MW00909112

Edited by Cheryl Whittier
Published by Autumn Day Publishing
Copyright 2016
Other works by L.S. Gagnon,
Witch: A New Beginning
Witch: The Spell Within
Witch: The Secret of the Leaves
Witch: The Final Chapter
Thea: The Little Witch, Into the Forest
Thea: The Little Witch, The Power of Believing
ISBN 978-0-9967707-1-2
All characters in this book are fiction
and figments of the author's imagination.

Thea: The Little Witch

Thea Goes to School

By L.S. Gagnon

A special thanks to Orion Gray, Odin Gray, and Raiden Gray. Thank you for inspiring my best characters yet. It was fun writing you into my books. I would also like to thank Toby Gray, who also happens to be an amazing illustrator. I would be lost without him. He and his wife, Leslie, have been nothing but welcoming to me.

Prologue

A child's mind is an endless ocean of dreams. They can reach for every star, follow every wish. Their untainted minds can show us a thing or two.

These were the best years of my life. It was a time when my innocence was untouched. A time when playing outside meant everything to me. My childhood taught me the meaning of true friends. I would carry these memories for the rest of my life.

Chapter One: Not Again

I sat by the window of our cottage, watching my friends, Cory and Delia, playing in the snow. They had been waiting for me all morning. Snowballs were being thrown, games were being played. I was taking no part in the fun; I found myself being kept in my little corner of the cottage, being punished—again.

I had really done it this time. My father was beyond angry with me. There was no fixing what I had done a few weeks ago. In my venture to find the real Santa Claus, I had messed things up real bad. To start with, I had kidnapped the wrong Santa Claus, or at least the man I thought was Santa Claus. Not only had I unknowingly kidnapped him, but I had also used my magic right in front of him, a rule I was *never* supposed to break.

Little witches like me were supposed to refrain from using our magic in front of humans. My wizard father always told me that humans would never understand how special I was, nor would they understand my magic. You see, I am half-wizard and half-witch, my mother being the witch. I don't need to cast spells like my mother. I can wave my hand to use my magic, just like my wizard father. He comes from a magical land where magic was born.

Kidnapping the wrong Santa wasn't the reason I was in trouble, although it should have been. No, I was in trouble because I had waved my hand and given Abigail, a little deaf human girl, her hearing back. The humans called it a Christmas miracle. I had forgotten I had even done that.

Sharron, a witch that lived next door, had quickly informed my father about it when she heard the humans talking about Abigail and how her hearing came back overnight. I could tell Sharron didn't want to rat me out—this time. She actually felt bad for having to tell my father. Sharron usually had no problem telling my father what I had done wrong. Just like Delia, Sharron was always moody and quick to point out what a problem child I was. But this time, she felt bad for getting me in trouble, not that it stopped her.

My father couldn't think of a way to fix my mistake without the humans taking notice. He had no choice but to stand back and hope for the best. Luckily, Abigail was only here visiting my human friends for Christmas. They had left town a few weeks ago; spreading the good news about a Christmas miracle in Salem. It took days for that news to settle down. All my father could do was hope they didn't suspect witches had done it.

Now I was back to being punished, back to my little corner of the cottage—again. Fortunately this time, my best friends, Cory and Delia were allowed to come over and visit if they wanted to. We would sit and talk about how we had met the *real* Santa Claus. That was another secret we couldn't share with our human friends. We had no idea how my father had found him, we only cared that he was in fact, real.

It turns out, Santa had no idea witches were real, either. That explained why we had never heard of him before. He felt bad for never visiting our home sooner, but promised to never forget us again. It would be a memory I would carry with me for the rest of my life.

"Thea, read your book," I heard my father say. "The snow will still be there tomorrow."

"But, winter is almost over," I whined. "I'll miss all the fun."

Slowly, my father's eyes shot up and glared at me. "Sit and read your book," he repeated.

"Yes, Father," I said, stepping away from the window.

Reading a few hours a day was part of my punishment. Every evening, I had to give my father a full report on what I had read. I didn't like his latest choice.

I pulled out a chair and sat next to him at the dinner table. As usual, he was deep into his own book. My father had been doing a lot of reading these days. He was determined to learn about every single holiday the humans celebrated. I heard him telling my mother that he didn't want any more surprises. *"Who knows what she'll do next,"* I heard him say.

I knew he was talking about me, of course. The minute I mentioned the Easter Bunny, my father had quickly done his research and read up on another human holiday called, Easter.

"Don't even think of bringing rabbits home," he'd warned.

I looked at the stack of books my father had in front of him. There must have been at least twenty of them. Was he going to read them all? How many holidays were there?

"Thea, read your book," he said again.

I sighed, pulling my own book toward me. The book was called, Utopia, a book my mother thought was too grown up for me.

"What page are you on?" my father asked, with his nose deep in his book.

My father looked wiser than any man I knew. His green eyes sparkled like two stars in the night. I never understood how humans could look upon him and not realize he was a wizard. There was something about my father that made him stand out. There was a certain glow about him. He radiated wisdom. All the witches, male and female, looked up to him. They all came to him for answers.

Dragging out the word *page*, my father asked, "What page, Thea?"

I didn't know what to answer. Truth was, I hadn't read a single page. I would only move my eyes along the pages when I thought my father was looking. I never imagined he would be asking me questions about it so soon.

Trying to think of what to say, I reached for my book. "Um," I said, flipping through the pages. "I think I lost my place."

My father's eyes peered from over the book he was holding. I nervously looked at him. He studied my eyes, slowly lowering his book.

"I see," he said, placing his book on the table. "Then tell me, what happened in chapter one?"

I looked down at the book. "Oh, I haven't gotten that far yet."

My father leaned back on his chair, crossing his arms in front of him. "Is that so? You *do* realize you've been reading that book for nine days, don't you?"

I swallowed thickly. I had to think of something fast. "I'm a very slow reader, Father. You really shouldn't rush me."

I heard my mother laughing over by the stove. She wore her long, brown hair down today. I thought it made her look younger when she wore it that way. My father loved to see her with her hair down. Sometimes he'd sit and stare at her the whole time she was cooking.

I bit my lip and looked at my father again. He glanced at my mother, a subtle smile on his face. "I'll tell you what, Thea," he said, rising to his feet. I'll give you until tomorrow to read twenty pages. If you cannot tell me what happened in those twenty pages, I will add four more weeks to your punishment."

"William," my mother said, stepping away from the stove. "You can't keep her a prisoner in this cottage. She needs air, for heaven's sake."

"I don't intend to," my father answered. "I never said her punishment would involve staying in this cottage."

His eyes slowly moved to me. "There are other ways of punishing her that will make her quite unhappy. Salem isn't the only place we can live."

What did he mean by that?

He picked up several books and told my mother he would be doing some reading outside. The moment he left, my mother gently grabbed my shoulders.

"Thea, why haven't you been reading the book? You understand why your father is upset with you, don't you?"

Again, I didn't answer. I had no excuse. How could I tell my mother that the only thing I could think of was playing outside? It killed me to see Cory and Delia having snowball fights without me. My mind couldn't concentrate on reading right now. I was too excited about the snow.

"You do know how to read, don't you?" my mother asked.

"Yes, Mother."

"Then why haven't you been reading? It's a fair punishment considering what you've done."

"But, Abigail couldn't hear," I pointed out.

"And, Abigail is also a human," my mother shot back. "Humans don't get their hearing back overnight. You could have put us all in danger, Thea. If we're discovered, we'll have to leave Salem. Don't you see that?"

Her words slowly flowed through my head. *Leave Salem?* How could we ever leave Salem? I loved it here. I couldn't imagine living anywhere else. I began to realize I was walking on thin ice. Now I understood what my father was talking about. He was threatening to move us.

"Think of Delia and Cory," my mother said softly. "You'd never see them again. You don't want that, do you?"

My heart sank. Panic began to travel through me. I loved my friends, and I would die without them. What had I done? I was digging a bigger hole for myself.

In a flash, I reached for the book, looked at my mother, and promised to read it.

"Twenty pages," she reminded me.

"I'll read fifty!" I assured her, and hurried to my room.

Chapter Two: Snowball

I had been reading for about an hour when my mother walked into my room. I was finding the book very confusing. Politics seemed to play a big part of it. My mother was right; this book was too grown up for me. I did *not* like it.

"Time to put the book down," she said, taking it from me. "You have some visitors."

I was more than happy to stop reading. I was even happier when I realized my visitors were my best friends, Cory and Delia. Cory lived next door with Sharron, the rat. Delia lived not far from here with her father, but he was never home, leaving Delia alone most of the time. I could tell my parents were not happy about that.

My friends were all bundled up in their winter clothes. Cory had red patches on his face from where Delia had nailed him with snowballs. I was missing all the fun. Delia was a rather moody witch, but I loved that about her. She had long, dark hair and dark eyes. Cory was tall and a few years older than me, but that never seemed to bother him.

"Why don't you join your friends outside," my mother suggested. "You can do some more reading when you come back."

Her words were music to my ears. In less than a second, I was putting on my coat and boots. I couldn't get out of the house fast enough.

"Are you still having snowball fights?" I asked my friends on the way out of the house.

"Yeah, but it's no fun without you," Cory answered. "Delia takes a long time to make her snowballs."

"Hey," Delia said offended. "I can't wave my hand like Thea. I actually have to touch the snow."

I smiled, knowing they had truly missed me. That was one good thing about being half-wizard. I was able to wave my hand and make dozens of snowballs in a matter of seconds. I would put spells in some of the snowballs, sometimes filling them with jam before I threw them. My mother would laugh when we'd walk in with purple faces and covered in jam.

When we stepped outside, I breathed in the cool winter air. Every inch of ground was covered in snow. It was the nice fluffy snow I liked so much. Sometimes the snow came down rather wet, making it heavy and useless for snowballs.

"Let's go invite Miri and her brothers," Cory suggested. "It can be us against them."

I quickly asked my mother if we could go invite my human friends to play. She agreed but said we had to come back and play here. "Your father doesn't want you going far," she reminded me.

"Yes, Mother."

As we made our way to Miri's house, Cory began telling me about a new family that had settled in Salem. I wasn't sure why that would interest him. New families moved here all the time. When he said, "I think they're witches," I understood why.

I was about to ask him why he thought they were witches when I spotted my father a few yards away. He was placing the books he had brought with him on a rock. He put them side by side before placing his hand over them.

"What is he doing?" Delia asked.

I motioned for her to stay quiet and hid behind some trees. We watched as my father closed his eyes and whispered, "Absorb."

I gasped when the book he was touching began to glow. Streams of light came out of the book and into my father's head. When the stream of light faded, he touched another book and did the same. "Absorb," he whispered.

I watched as my father touched all the books. I was trying to understand what he was doing when Delia whispered, "He's using magic to read them."

"That's what it looks like," Cory agreed.

Boy, what a cheater my father was. Why hadn't he shared his way of reading books with me? I could have finished that boring book in seconds.

"That's a good trick to know," Cory said. "I wish I could do that."

"Someone like Thea could do that," Delia pointed out. "I bet she could read a hundred books in a matter of seconds."

Cory's eyes lit up. "Hey, let's go find some books."

"No," I whined. "I want to have a snowball fight. Spring will be here soon and I've hardly played in the snow."

As usual, Delia rolled her eyes. "Oh please, Thea. You've been out plenty of times and played."

"Not every day," I was quick to remind her.

"Whose there?" I heard my father say.

Without another word, we ran into the trees and out of sight. There was no way I was going to let my father see me. He would no doubt send me back home to read.

We didn't stop running until we arrived at Miri's house. I was disappointed when her mother said she wasn't home. "She's in school, Sweetie. Shouldn't the three of you also be in school?" she asked.

I didn't like when Miri's mother asked us questions. We never knew what to answer.

"Oh, our school is closed," I lied. "We don't have to be there right now."

Truth was, we had no idea what school was. Miri had explained that it was a place where you learned things. The three of us had been talking about it for weeks. We wanted to find out what Miri was learning.

"Are you still on vacation?" Miri's mother asked. "I thought Christmas vacation was over weeks ago."

Miri's mother gave us a strange look when we wouldn't answer. "What is the name of your school again?" she asked.

I swallowed nervously. We were done for. I had no answer to give. She had no way of knowing that witches didn't go to school. My father had taught us how to read and write many years ago, but I couldn't tell her that. I just wish she would stop asking us questions.

"You *do* go to school, don't you?" the mother asked, leaning toward us. "What grades are you in?"

Confused, Cory asked, "Grades?"

"Yes, what year of school are you in?"

"This year," I answered hoping that was the right answer.

"Is that a question, or an answer?" the mother asked.

"Definitely an answer," Delia quickly said. "We are this year in school."

We all nodded, happy with our response.

I didn't like the suspicious look Miri's mother was giving us. It was like she was trying to figure something out. "Tell me again, where did you meet my children?"

Her eyes were full of doubt. The smile she had greeted us with was all but gone. She wanted answers from us.

I felt Delia reach for my hand and squeeze it. Although Miri and her brothers knew we were witches, they had kept that secret from their parents. Zachary, Miri's brother, had lied and said we went to another school. He explained to his mother that we had met while begging for treats, which was not a lie.

I thought I would pass out as Miri's mother waited for our answer. Was she putting the puzzle together? Could she tell we were witches? Better yet, would she make Miri stay away from us because of it?

"Who is your teacher?" the mother asked. "I know most of the teachers in this area. Maybe I know your teacher."

Now she wanted names. We were done for. I thought about running, but that would only make her grow more suspicious.

"What do we do?" Delia whispered.

I looked into the mother's eyes. They were drilling into me, waiting for an answer. In a moment of panic, I blurted out the words… "We're not witches, I swear."

"What?" the mother asked confused.

In that very moment, I knew it was time to run. My boots couldn't get me out of there fast enough. I broke into a run with Cory and Delia right behind me.

"Did you say witches?" I heard the mother yell.

Chapter Three: In Ten Minutes?

We ran like our lives depended on it. What just happened? Did I just tell Miri's mother that we were witches? Did those words really come out of my mouth?

"You really did it this time," Delia said, feeling the need to remind me.

"I know!" I said, running faster.

It was so hard to run in the snow. Cory kept picking me up when I would get stuck.

"Is she behind us?" Delia asked, looking over her shoulder.

I almost screamed when someone scooped me off my feet. I knew I was done for when I heard Delia and Cory gasp. It was my father.

"Why are you running?" he asked.

My heart was racing as he looked around for the danger. He held me close to him as he tried to figure out who was chasing us.

"Is someone after you?" he asked, looking in every direction.

I did the only thing I knew how to do best. I began to cry.

My father quickly put me on my feet and began checking every inch of me.

"Where are you hurt?" he asked in a panic.

"I only wanted to have a snowball fight," I cried. "I didn't mean it, I swear."

"Thea, what are you talking about?" my father asked, grabbing my shoulders.

I looked into his eyes, terrified at what he may do to me.

"You'll punish me some more," I sobbed.

Frustrated, he looked at Cory for answers. Cory didn't miss a beat. He told my father everything. I knew he had no choice. When Cory was done, my father gave me a death stare.

"In Thea's defense," Cory added. "None of us knew what to answer the woman."

"She was asking so many questions," Delia chimed in.

My father nodded and rose to his feet.

"Take Thea home. I'll take care of it."

"Yes. Sir," Cory said, grabbing my hand.

My father headed toward Miri's house. I cried all the way back to the cottage. There was no telling how long my father was going to add to my punishment. Delia and Cory would be old by the time I saw them again. And with that thought, I cried some more.

"Why is she crying?" my mother asked, running to my side.

"She's in trouble—again," Delia quickly announced.

"What?" my mother asked confused. "How can she be in trouble? She just left."

Cory began to relay the story. All I could do was bite my lip. "William is taking care of it," Cory explained.

My mother sighed and looked down at me.

"Thea, in ten minutes, really?"

"I think she broke a record," Delia laughed.

My mother shot her a look. "This isn't funny, young lady."

We all waited for my father just outside the cottage. I began to realize I should have made a final wish list. Where would my friends scatter my ashes? Would they want to bury me instead?

When my father came walking out of the woods, I stopped breathing.

"How did it go?" my mother quickly asked.

"She won't remember a thing," my father assured her.

I knew my wizard father had erased the woman's memory. Those were the kind of powers a wizard like him had. I knew Miri's mother would never remember my visit.

I bit my lip again as my father looked down at me.

"I'm not angry with you, Thea," he said.

"You're not?" I asked a little shocked.

He smiled. "Those were some tough questions for someone like you. Considering that you have no idea what school is, I understand why you ran."

"You do?"

He nodded. "I also think it's time the three of you learn what school is."

"What do you mean?" my mother asked.

My father smiled at her. "I can't home school them forever. They need to be around other children their age. Even you pointed that out, did you not?"

"We're home schooled?" Cory asked confused.

"What is that?" I asked.

My father looked at the three of us. "Do you know how to read?"

We all nodded.

"And, who taught you how to write?"

"You did," Delia answered.

He smiled. "That would make me your teacher. What human children learn in *school*, I have been teaching you at home. You've always gone to school, you just didn't know it."

I began to think of all the times my father sat the three of us down with his books. It was true, he did teach us all those things. I even knew about numbers and how to add them up. I was beginning to understand what school was. Miri was right, it really was a place where you learned things, and I was just learning those things at home.

"There is one thing I can't teach you," my father continued. "I can't teach you about human habits. And as we all know, that's why Thea has gotten into so much trouble."

Everyone eyed me.

"What are you saying?" my mother asked.

He sighed. "I'm saying, I think it's time the three of them went to a human school."

My mother didn't look happy about that. She kept looking at me and shaking her head.

"William, what if she says something about who she is? You know how impulsive she can be."

My father laughed. "Thea knows she shouldn't tell people that she's a witch, but somehow, those words seem to keep coming out of her mouth."

"They sure do," Cory laughed with him.

"William," my mother said sounding concerned. "This isn't funny. What if she slips again? The whole town will know we're witches."

He held up his hand. "I've already thought of that, Emma. I assure you, those words will not come out of her mouth."

"How can you be certain?" she asked.

A big smile spread across his face. "I'm a wizard, my dear. Have faith that I will take care of things."

My mother wasn't convinced. She kept looking at me with worry in her eyes. My father noticed and quickly gathered her in his arms.

"Emma, you've told me many times that Thea needs to be around human children. This will be good for her. She can learn what we can't teach her. Humans come closer to us with each passing day. Soon, she will have to live among them. She must learn to understand them."

My mother glanced at me again. "She'll be fine," my father assured her.

My mother thought about it for several long moments. "If you think it will help," she finally said.

"So, we have to lie about who we really are?" Cory asked.

My parents exchanged glances. My mother gave my father a knowing look. "See what you started," she said to him.

My father sighed. "Come inside," he said to the three of us. "We need to talk."

Chapter Four: The Spell

We all removed our coats as my father sat at the table. My mother grabbed some wood and started a fire. I knew she was about to make some tea. Maybe she would offer us some of her delicious biscuits.

"Sit down," my father said to us.

We all pulled out a chair as we watched my mother start the tea. Cory's eyes lit up when my mother put some butter on the table. We knew her biscuits would be next.

My father tapped on the table when the three of us wouldn't look away from my mother.

"I'm going to teach you the difference between lying, and keeping a secret," he said.

"I've never lied to you," Delia said, a bit offended.

"Yeah, me either," Cory added.

They both looked at me. I bit my lip. "Um, I don't lie. I just withhold information."

"Enough," my father said. "What I have to say is very important."

We all sat in silence. "Have any of you ever kept a secret?" my father asked.

All at once, my friends turned to look at me. My father rolled his eyes. "I mean an important secret. Not one Thea told you to keep from me," he said, eyeing me.

"You mean, like the Santa Claus secret?" Delia asked.

"Yes, just like the Santa secret," my father answered. "Well, I need you to keep another secret. And to make sure you don't tell anyone, I'm going to put a spell on you."

"A spell?" my mother asked, placing some biscuits on the table. "What kind of spell, William?"

He looked up at her. "I'm going to make sure the word, 'witch' never leaves their lips."

"I'll never tell anyone we're witches," Cory said, reaching for a biscuit. I didn't miss the glance he gave *me* when he said that.

"I'm afraid I can't take that chance," my father answered. He reached for a biscuit and asked Cory to pass the butter. "I won't ask you to lie," he said, taking the butter from Cory. "but I will make sure you keep our secret."

Again, glances came my way.

"It will make me feel better about sending you to school," my father explained.

Cory and Delia looked me again. "And the word, 'witch' will never leave our lips?" Cory asked.

My father laughed. "I give you my word."

"I want proof," Delia demanded.

My father smiled. "I can understand that, young lady."

Why did everyone keep looking my way?

My mother poured us some tea as we enjoyed her buttery biscuits. It was her best batch yet. When we were done eating, my father rose to his feet. "Are we ready?" he asked.

"You're casting the spell now?" Cory asked.

My father nodded.

"Close your eyes," he instructed.

I quickly bowed my head and closed my eyes. I took a quick peek to see if Cory and Delia were doing the same thing. "We're ready," Delia said, squeezing her eyes shut.

I kept my eyes closed as I heard my father's steps. I felt my body tingle when he tapped me on the head. My head felt funny for a moment, but it quickly went away when I opened my eyes.

"Did you do it?" I asked.

He smiled. "The deed is done."

I don't feel any different," Delia said, touching her head.

"Yeah, me either," Cory added.

"Thea," my father said, looking down at me. "What are you?"

Confused by the question, I answered, "A girl."

"No, I mean what are you? What is your mother?"

I looked at my mother knowing the answer. I wanted to say, witch, but my mouth wouldn't let me say the word. "A woman," I said instead.

And you, Delia?" my father asked. "What are you?"

"Confused," she answered.

He laughed. "Can any of you say the word, witch?"

As much as I tried, that word would not come out of my mouth. "Wrinkle," I managed to say.

"Water," Cory said next.

"Wood," Delia spat out. "Hey," she said, looking up at my father. "That's not what I wanted to say."

My parents looked at each other. "This may just work," my mother said, seeming less nervous.

Again, my father smiled. "I'll have to find out what we need to do to get them put into this place called, *school*."

He began to make his way to the door.

"Where are you going?" my mother asked.

"I'm going to pay that woman a visit again. I'm sure I can get the information I need from her memories. It's not like I can just ask her."

I instantly knew he was going to Miri's house again. I knew my father was about to read her mother's mind to get all the answers he needed. I looked at my mother, who looked plenty worried again.

"Wait here," she said, as she followed my father out of the house.

"Why now?" I heard her ask.

We all rushed to the window so we could see what was going on. "Stay quiet, so we can hear them." I wanted to hear every word.

With a concerned look on his face, my father turned and faced her. "They're everywhere, Emma. Soon, we won't be able to avoid all the humans. We need to teach our children how to live among them. You were right, I can't hide her forever."

I watched my father disappear into the woods. My mother stood, clutching her heart.

"We're really going to school," Cory said.

"What are we going to do there?" Delia asked.

"Learn stuff," I said, stepping away from the window. "Miri says they learn something new every day."

At that moment, I knew who could answer our questions. It was time to find Miri and her brothers.

Chapter Five: New in Town

We quickly asked my mother if we could go out and play. She was still staring into the trees.

"Don't be long," she said, seeming lost in thought.

We ran into the forest, looking behind us to make sure my mother was out of ear shot.

"Where are we going?" Cory asked.

"Miri and her brothers will be passing through here soon," I explained. "We can ask them our questions about school."

"That's not for hours," Delia pointed out. "What are we going to do until then?"

I gave her question some thought. "Why don't we go see these new magical people Cory told us about?" I suggested.

I was surprised when the words, *magical people*, came out of my mouth instead of *witches*. My father's spell was really working.

"Magical people?" Delia laughed.

"You try saying whimper," I answered.

The word *witch* still would not come out of my mouth.

"They don't live far from here," Cory informed us. "We could be there in no time."

We all agreed and began to make our way towards their house. "So how do you know they're magical?" I asked.

Cory shrugged his shoulders. "I'm not sure, but they look like wishers."

Delia rolled her eyes. "Just say, magical. We obviously can't say the word…" She began to spell out the word, *witch,* in the air.

"Magical it is," Cory answered.

We began walking again. "You mean you're not sure if they're *magical*?" I asked.

Cory nodded. "So what makes you think they're like us?" Delia asked.

"I don't know," he answered. "They just look magical. There are three of them, all boys. They don't dress like the humans, or even look like them."

"So that makes them magical?" Delia asked.

~ 33 ~

"You'll understand when you see them," Cory answered.

We made our way through the woods until we reached a narrow brook. I had seen this brook before. Delia and I came here often in the summer to get our feet wet. Sometimes, the brook carried a lot of water, making it possible for Delia and me to swim and play in it.

I looked at the old house that had been empty for quite some time. I had always thought it was abandoned. Now the place looked like someone was working on it. It looked very much lived in. Near the house was an open stable with an old carriage inside. The carriage looked like it hadn't been used in years. I spotted ropes hanging from a tree; with a small piece of old wood that made it a swing.

Several chickens were running around the massive yard. There was a vegetable garden near some more swings. I spotted a little wooden bridge that someone had built to cross the brook.

"Look," Cory said, pointing. "It's a little house in a tree."

"It's called a treehouse," Delia said, rolling her eyes.

"Wow," I said amazed. "This place was made for children."

I actually liked this place. It was surrounded with huge pine trees. There was so much space to run and have fun here. I decided to venture into the yard.

"Where are you going?" Cory said, grabbing my arm.

"I'm going to look around. It doesn't seem like anyone is home."

"I don't know," Cory said, looking toward the house.

"I want to climb into that treehouse," Delia said, running out of the bushes.

Cory tried to stop us, but it was too late. Delia and I were climbing up the tree within moments.

"We can throw snow balls at Cory from up here," I said excitedly. "His snowballs will never be able to reach us."

I was almost near the entrance of the treehouse when I heard Delia, who was ahead of me, let out a loud gasp. Cory was running out from the trees within seconds. "What's wrong?" he yelled.

I had to gently push Delia out of the way so I could look inside. "You're blocking my way," I said, making my way through.

As soon as I looked inside, I realized why Delia had gasped. Sitting inside the treehouse, eyes wide open, were three little boys. Clearly they didn't know what to make of us.

They were obviously brothers. The oldest, looked to be about twelve years old. The middle one, looked like he was about ten. The youngest, and the most shocked, looked to be around eight. They looked so much like each other that I could hardly tell them apart.

The three boys were very handsome. They had long, dark brown hair with beautiful eyes that had a certain slant to them. Their skin was a honey brown, and their faces revealed features that were strong and rugged. I found them to have a very exotic look that now held all of my attention.

The oldest boy slowly rose to his feet. The other two quickly stood behind him.

"What do you want?" the oldest boy asked.

Before I could answer, Cory made his way up the tree and into the treehouse. He froze when he saw the boys.

I couldn't help but notice the youngest had a rope tied around his waist. The middle boy was holding the other end of the rope.

"Is he your prisoner?" I asked.

The oldest gave me a confused look.

"What? No," he said, shaking his head. "He's my little brother."

"So why do you keep a rope around him?" I asked.

He ignored my question. "Who are you, and what do you want?"

Cory stepped forward. "I'm very sorry. We shouldn't be here. They only wanted to see the treehouse."

"I'm Thea," I said, stepping around Cory. "This is Delia, and Cory. They are my best friends."

"Should we call for father?" the middle boy asked.

"Stay quiet, Odin," the older boy told him.

"Odin?" I said with a big smile. "I've never heard that name before."

"My name is Raiden," the youngest boy said. "And his name is Orion," he said, pointing at the oldest brother.

"Raiden, be quiet," Orion hissed.

"We heard you were new in town," I said, moving a bit closer. "We came to welcome you."

They only gave us nervous looks.

"Don't be scared," I said, trying to calm them. "We're not going to hurt you."

Orion looked at his brothers. "We're not going to hurt you, either," he said, looking back at me.

"Of course not," I said, moving closer to them. "This is a very nice treehouse you have. I've never seen one before."

"My father built it for us," Raiden answered from behind his brother.

I looked at the youngest again. "Raiden, is it?" He nodded. "Why do you have a rope around your waist?"

Odin, the middle brother, started laughing.

"He likes to stray away a lot," he explained. "We have to keep him close by so he doesn't get lost."

"We should get one of those for Thea," Delia teased.

Orion, the oldest, still seemed very nervous.

"You really shouldn't be here," he said. "We're not supposed to talk to strangers."

"Can we be friends, then?" I asked. "You have a really nice yard. I bet we could play lots of games."

"Yeah, let's go play some games," the youngest said.

Orion quickly picked up a cup of what looked like water. "Here," he said, handing it to his little brother. "Just drink your water. Don't say another word."

What was wrong with him? Why didn't he want to be friends?

"Come on, Thea," Cory said, grabbing my hand. "We shouldn't be here."

I leaned in to whisper in Cory's ear. "I don't think they're magical," I said to him.

Cory nodded. "Yeah, I think you're right."

"It was nice to meet you," I said. "I'm sorry we scared you."

"We didn't mean to scare you, either," Orion answered.

"Oh, I'm not scared," I assured him.

"You're not?" he asked shocked.

"Why would I be?"

He swallowed hard and looked at his brothers again. "You'd better go now," he said, motioning toward the entrance.

It took us only moments to climb down from the tree. We quickly made our way back into the woods. "They were very odd," Delia said. "No wonder Cory thought they were magical."

"I would have bet my life on it," Cory added.

"They seem very nice," I said. "I hope we see them again."

"I think we have enough human friends," Cory said, pulling me behind him.

Chapter Six: Books

By the time we arrived back to the cottage, we had missed Miri and her brothers. My questions would have to wait.

We walked into the cottage to find my father gathering up some books. There were three bags in front of him. He seemed to be deciding what books to place in each of the bags.

"And, you say you couldn't tell what kind of books they were carrying?" my mother was asking.

My father shook his head. "They seem to bring books with them. I'm just not sure what kind of books."

"Pack one of each," my mother suggested. "One of them is bound to be the right one."

"I suppose your right," my father said, stuffing more books into the bags.

My father spun around when he realized we were home. "Ah, just in time," he said, putting yet another book into each of the bags. "You'll need to clean yourselves up," he ordered. "I want all of you to take baths tonight. Delia, you are staying here tonight."

"Is my father not home?" Delia asked.

"As usual," my mother said through her teeth.

"I don't understand that man," my father grumbled under his breath. "She's just a child."

My mother instructed Cory to bring her some of his clothes. "I'll have to do some sewing," she said.

Cory was off in a flash. My mother began to hold dresses up to me and Delia. "I think I can make these look newer," she said, sizing them up.

My father began to gather wood to heat up some water. He usually left the house when I had to take a bath. We had a small, wooden tub in the corner of the cottage.

After Delia and I had taken our bath, my father said he wanted to speak with us. Cory was already waiting outside.

"You can come in now," my mother called to him.

The three of us sat and looked up at my father, waiting to see what he had to say.

He sighed. "I want you to know that I'm doing this for your own good. I want you to pay attention, and listen to whatever the teacher says. Emma and I will bring you to school tomorrow. We will also be waiting when you get out. Do you understand?"

We all nodded.

He sighed again and continued. "Although they may teach you things you may already know, I don't want you telling the teacher that. Take in any information she's willing to teach you. It's important that you fit in with the humans. Watch them, learn from them. Don't do anything strange around them, and most importantly, do not let them know you are witches."

He was looking right at me.

"As of tomorrow," he continued. "You will act and live as a human. Do you understand?"

Again, we all nodded.

"If by chance, should any of you give away what you are," he said, looking at me again. "your punishment will be severe. This will be your only warning."

I quickly swallowed down my fear. He meant business. I couldn't mess things up this time.

"I'll be good, Father. I promise."

He knelt down, grabbing my hand. "You have to be careful, Thea. This is very important to us. Soon, humans will be all around us. You must learn as much as you can from them. One day, you'll be living in their world."

"I understand, Father."

He smiled. "I know you won't disappoint me." He rose to his feet. "One more thing, and it's the most important thing of all. Absolutely no magic—ever! No spells, no magic, no excuses. Do you all understand?"

"Yes," we all answered at once.

When my father was done with his talk, my mother served us an early dinner. Cory, Delia, and I sat around talking about school. "What does it look like?" Delia asked.

"I don't know," I answered. "But I bet it's beautiful. Why else would children want to go every day?"

"Miri and her brothers said you can even play there," Cory chimed in. "Imagine, a place where we can play *and* learn stuff."

"I can't wait," I said excitedly.

"I wonder what Miri will say when she sees us." Delia said. "You think she'll be happy?"

"Why wouldn't she?" I answered. "Miri loves us."

We spent the rest of the evening talking about school. I knew the night was going to seem long. I couldn't wait to go there. I had made up my mind to behave myself. I would not give my father any reason to worry. I planned on making him proud. The pressure was on. I didn't want to disappoint him.

By the time Cory headed home, I was ready for bed. I climbed in bed right next to Delia. She seemed a little sad. I caught her staring into space a few times tonight.

"Are you okay?" I asked.

She pulled the blankets over herself. "I'm fine. I just miss my father."

I didn't know what to say. It broke my heart to know she was alone most of the time.

I lay on my side and faced her. "When was the last time you saw him?" I asked.

She closed her eyes, tears spilling over. "It was weeks ago," she admitted. "Even then, he was only home for about an hour. He didn't even talk to me much, either. It was like I wasn't even there."

She wiped her tears away. "Do you suppose he doesn't love me?"

I never answered her question. I didn't want to lie to her. Of course I thought he didn't love her. If he did, he would never leave her alone so much.

I had once overheard my mother and father talking about him. My father said he often saw him in town, and always drunk. It broke my heart to know Delia had a father like that.

I wrapped my arms around Delia as she cried herself to sleep. I caught my father looking into my room, staring at Delia. "She's lucky to have you," he whispered to me.

I didn't sleep very well that night. I felt an overwhelming need to take Delia's pain away. I wanted to help her, make her feel loved. There had to be something I could do. And with that thought, I finally slipped into my dreams.

Chapter Seven: Oily Hair

I stretched my arms, yawning as the sunlight softly filled my room. I was surprised to see that Delia was already out of bed. I sat up and inhaled my mother's cooking. "Breakfast," my mother called. "Are you awake, Thea?"

I wanted to laugh the moment I walked out of my room. Cory was sitting at the table; it looked like a cow had licked one side of his head.

"Don't even think about it," he warned, when he noticed I was staring.

He knew I was about to tease him.

My mother cleared her throat. "Thea, doesn't Cory look handsome? Sharron was kind enough to help him get ready for school."

Delia had her hand over her mouth, trying not to laugh.

"She put some kind of oil in my hair," Cory said, looking down at his plate.

"Did she use the whole can?" I asked.

"Thea!" my mother yelled.

Cory's hair was parted to one side. It was slick and stuck to his head. I think I even saw streams of oil running down his forehead.

"Morning," Sharron said, almost dancing through the door. "I packed a lunch," she said, handing Cory a bag.

My father was right behind her. He did a double take when he saw Cory.

"Doesn't he look handsome?" my mother said, giving my father a look.

He looked at Sharron, who was beaming with pride. She pulled on her curly, brown hair as she waited for my father's approval.

"Um, yes," my father answered. "Well done, Sharron."

Sharron smiled. "I wanted him to look normal. You know, like the humans."

"Humans cover their heads in oil?" I asked.

"Thea!" my mother yelled again.

Cory jumped to his feet. "I'll wait outside," he said, storming out.

I thought Cory's hair was the worst of it. I hadn't seen what he was wearing. I tried not to laugh at his pants. They were two sizes too small for him, and too short. I tried to look away as he slipped on his coat, but I just couldn't get past his shiny shoes. Sharron had really done a number on him.

"You're not putting oil in my hair, are you?" I asked my mother.

My father tried his best not to laugh. I could see his shoulders bouncing up and down as he looked away.

My mother glanced at Sharron and quickly cleared her throat. "We should be on our way, William."

My father nodded; his face red from trying to hold in his laughter. "Y…yes, of course."

I finished my breakfast and quickly slipped on the dress my mother had patched up for me. My mother brushed my hair first, and then Delia's.

"The two of you behave yourselves, you hear me?" she said, handing me my coat.

My father called for us to hurry. He was holding our book bags when we walked outside. I could see that Cory was having a hard time holding up his. When my father handed me my bag, it hit the ground with a thud.

"Did you pack rocks in there?" I asked, peaking into the bag.

"I'll have to drag mine," Delia said, trying to pick hers up.

Frustrated, my father picked up my bag. "I was afraid of that."

He put my bag in front of him and instructed Cory and Delia to put their bags next to mine.

"What are you going to do?" my mother asked.

"I'll have to take some of the books out. Perhaps by the end of the day they will tell us what books they really need."

Sharron quickly went through Cory's bag. She took out three books and handed them to my father. When my bag was lighter, my father handed it back to me.

"Try it now," he said.

The bag still felt a little heavy, but it wasn't so bad that I couldn't carry it.

"Better," I lied. I didn't want to tell my father that it was still heavy. He had gone through so much trouble picking out the books.

Sharron wished us well and headed back to her cottage. My mother grabbed her coat and we were on our way.

The three of us talked excitedly as my father and mother walked behind us.

"They're going to laugh at me," Cory was saying. "I look like a fool."

"Yeah, and your collar is full of oil, too" I pointed out.

"Enough, Thea," my mother yelled.

My father came to a sudden stop. "Just one second," he said, looking around.

He looked in every direction possible.

"What are you looking for?" my mother asked.

"Human eyes," my father answered.

When the coast was clear, he looked at Cory and gave him a big smile. "I'll have to put things back to normal before you go home and Sharron sees you," he said.

"Back to normal?" Cory asked confused.

With one wave of my father's hand, Cory's pants lengthened and got bigger. My father looked at Cory's hair and waved his hand again. In an instant, the oil was all but gone. Cory's hair fell across his face again.

"Oh, thank you," Cory said relieved.

"It will be our little secret," my father said, giving Cory a pat on the back.

We began walking again. We stopped when we heard someone behind us.

"It's Miri!" Delia sang.

I spun around. It really was her. Zachary and Aidan were with her. They were my human friends. I couldn't believe we would be walking to school together.

Miri didn't seem surprised to see us.

"Little Witch, what are you doing here?" she asked, giving my father a glance.

I pitched my chin up and announced proudly, "We're going to school."

"You are?"

Cory said hello to Zachary and Aidan.

"Since when do witches go to school?" Miri asked.

"Since today," I answered. "But you can't call me winner, okay?"

"Winner?" Miri asked confused.

"You know, magical."

"You mean, witch?" Miri corrected me.

My father quickly explained to Miri what was going on. "She can't say the word, 'witch', even if she tried."

Miri laughed. "I understand," she said to him. "That was very smart of you."

I couldn't get over how much Miri had grown. I looked like a little girl standing next to her. I remember I used to be taller than her. Even her brothers had grown a bit.

I looked at my mother. I know I had promised her I wouldn't ask why my father was keeping me the same age. I just couldn't understand his reasons. It was then I noticed that Delia and Cory were also shorter than our human friends. Was my father also keeping them the same age?

"We're going to be late," my father said, leading the way.

Chapter Eight: School

My heart came alive when we emerged from the forest. It wasn't very often that my parents brought me into town with them. I loved coming here. I thought the little town was beautiful. I loved to watch the different carriages going by. I would sit and stare at all the humans while my mother did her shopping.

There were humans everywhere. It was the one place that made my mother very nervous. She usually did her shopping as quickly as she could and got out of there. Humans scared her, and it wasn't because humans were bad people. She knew that witches were not welcomed here. She had even known a few witches that were discovered and jailed, just for being a witch. Most of them, my mother always said, were fine human beings.

I could see the worry in my mother's eyes as two humans walked by us. She looked down at me and bit her lip. "Are you sure about this, William?" she said, grabbing my father's hand.

"They'll be fine," he assured her. "I'll stay close by."

My mother held my father's hand until we reached a big house. There were human children of all ages, playing outside.

"Do they all live there?" I asked.

Miri laughed. "Thea, that's our school."

I looked at the house again. I was expecting something else. I thought it would be more grand or something. It was off white in color and very small, with a metal bell hanging on its porch. The windows to the school were small, but there were a lot of them. Then I saw an open field where more human children were playing.

"That's the playground," Miri said when she noticed I was looking in that direction.

"They have a special ground to play on?" Delia asked amazed.

Zachary and Aidan quickly left to join their friends. Cory seemed disappointed that Zachary hadn't asked him to come with them.

"See you in class," Zachary said over his shoulder.

"Where are they going?" I asked. "And, where is this class?

Miri shook her head. "Class is inside the school, Thea. It's a room where we all sit and learn."

"Come," my father said, taking my hand. "We should introduce ourselves to the teacher."

We crossed the street and made our way to the school. As we walked up onto the porch, I noticed my father taking in a deep breath. He stopped at the door, took another deep breath, and walked in.

I scanned the room called, *class*. Cory and Delia were also taking it all in. There were long wooden tables covering every inch available. I spotted a smaller table at the top of the room. There was an older woman sitting behind it. A strange looking wall was behind her. It was dark in color and had words all over it.

The woman had her head down and was writing with some kind of feather. *Why was she using a feather?* Her grey hair was pinned up in a bun. Her dress had a very high collar. It almost came up to her chin. She didn't look very friendly.

"Is that the teacher?" Delia whispered to me.

I shrugged my shoulders and looked at the woman. "Are you the teacher?" I yelled.

The woman almost dropped the feather when I said that. She pushed her chair back and rose to her feet. "Young lady," she hissed. "We do not yell in this classroom."

My father pinched my arm and apologized to the angry woman. Miri walk out laughing and said she was going to look for her friends.

"I'll see you in a bit," she said, waving.

The angry woman made her way over to us.

"What do we have here?" she said, looking down at us. "Are you my new students?"

I wasn't sure what to say. "Um, we came here so you can teach us stuff, even though we may already know it."

I felt my father's grip get a little tighter around my wrist as he quickly explained, "What she meant to say is that they are eager to learn."

The woman nodded and looked down at us again. "I expect nothing less from my students. I do not tolerate laziness. You will pay attention and do as you're told. Do I make myself clear?"

I looked at Cory and Delia. I knew they were thinking the same thing I was—was she related to Sharron?

"I assure you," my father said. "They will not give you any trouble."

"Good," she said, pulling on her collar. "I also do not tolerate tardiness. I expect my students to be on time and ready to learn."

I couldn't look away from her beady eyes and long pointed nose. Her mouth was big, with horrible yellow looking teeth. Her raspy voice was irritating to the ears.

I jumped back when she looked at me. Her eyes traveled the length of my body and down to my shoes. Her glare slowly moved to Delia and Cory. "Are these the clothes you expect them to attend school with?" she asked, looking back at my father.

My mother instantly became offended. "And what is wrong with their clothes? I spent all night patching them up."

The woman raised an eyebrow. "I have standards. I expect my students clean and properly dressed."

My mother moved closer to her. "I will repeat my question. What is wrong with their clothes?"

Before the woman could answer, I saw three familiar faces walking in. It was the boys from the treehouse, Orion, Odin, and Raiden. They looked just as nervous as we did. Delia elbowed me and pointed to their clothes. I quickly noticed patches all over their pants.

"The teacher hates patches," I whispered to her.

The man standing behind them had long hair just like them. He had the same slanted eyes and honey brown skin. *Must be their father*, I thought.

I quickly noticed that they were each holding a wooden cup in their hands. I wanted to laugh when I saw that Raiden still had the rope tied around his waist, and his brother Odin still had a hold of the other end.

"Are you the teacher?" Raiden yelled.

I couldn't help but laugh.

"Young man," the woman said, stepping away from us. "We do not yell in this classroom."

"Where do we go to yell, then?" Raiden asked.

Delia and I burst into laughter. The woman snapped her head around. I composed myself the moment her beady eyes met mine.

"I see I will also be teaching these children some manners," she said, walking back to her table.

"Take a seat anywhere," she commanded, waving toward the tables. "I'll be sounding the bell soon."

"Do you need anything from us?" my father asked.

"Yes," she said, not bothering to look up. "I need you to leave."

I couldn't help but notice the look my parents gave each other.

"Go sit down, Thea," my father said, gently pushing me away.

Cory, Delia and I sat together. I looked at the boys. They looked unsure about whether to sit or not. Their father squatted down. "We talked about this, boys. You said you would give it a try."

Orion, the oldest, gave the teacher a glare.

"How long do we have to stay?" he asked his father.

"Class ends promptly at three," the woman answered from her table.

The father nodded and looked at his boys. "Stay close to each other. Remember what we talked about. Don't forget to drink your water. Make sure your brother never takes off that rope."

Orion nodded.

"I said... sit," the angry woman said.

I smiled when the boys came to sit at our table. Raiden, the youngest, softy said, "I don't like her."

"Be quiet," Orion muttered.

We all looked at our parents. They didn't seem to want to leave. Even the boys' father was still there. They looked nervous as they looked at the angry woman, and back at us.

"Remember what we talked about," my father said.

He gave the stern woman a last glance as he and my mother walked out. The boy's father also gave her a glance. He nervously waved at his sons and made his way out.

"Why can't we just go out and play?" Raiden asked his oldest brother.

"We have to stay here," Orion answered.

He grabbed the wooden cup and handed it to Raiden. "Here, drink your water."

The angry woman shot her head up. "There will be no drinking in this classroom," she said, pushing her chair back.

She quickly made her way to our table.

"I'll take these," she said, reaching for the wooden cups.

I was surprised when Orion put his hands over the cups and stopped her.

"Don't touch our cups," he hissed.

"We need that water," Odin said, getting to his feet. "Our father said we had to drink it."

The angry woman straightened herself. Her beady eyes glared down at him. "There is a well out back if you become thirsty. I do not tolerate drinks in my classroom."

"But, he's parched," I pointed out.

The woman snatched the cups up and emptied the water out the window. I thought the boys were going to have a panic attack. They looked like they had lost their best friend.

"I'll keep these until class is over," she said, shoving the wooden cups behind her table.

Orion, the oldest, pulled his brother back. "Just sit down," Orion said, giving the teacher another glare.

The teacher walked outside to the porch and began to hit the bell with small metal rod. Within moments, the room was filled with human children.

I looked at Delia and Cory. "Here we go," I said, putting my book bag on the table.

Chapter Nine: Class

I was disappointed when Miri didn't sit with us. I thought she would be more excited to see me here. I was hoping she would be showing us around the ground that they put aside for us to play on. Cory watched Zachary and Aidan sit with their friends at the back of the room. I wasn't the only one who noticed the changes in them.

We all looked forward when the teacher stood at the front of the room. She clamped her hands behind her back and looked at everyone with her beady eyes.

"We have some new students this morning," she began. "I will expect you to educate them on all our rules."

She put one hand up and motioned for us to stand. "Give the class your names," she ordered.

I went first. "My name is Thea."

"I'm Delia."

"Cory."

"My name is Orion, and these are my brothers…"

"They can say their own names, if you don't mind," the teacher cut in.

Orion looked at his brothers and nodded.

"I'm Odin."

"And, I'm thirsty," Raiden said, pulling on his brother's arm.

The humans erupted into laughter. "Nice to meet you, *Thirsty*," one boy said.

Again, the room was filled with laughter.

"Enough!" the teacher yelled.

Within seconds, the room was silent.

"You may sit now," she said to us.

As we were taking our seats, the teacher noticed Raiden's rope. She quickly told the boys to get back up. "Why is there a rope around his waist?" she demanded to know. "Take it off, at once."

"We can't. He'll run away from us?" Orion explained.

I felt bad when the humans laughed again.

"Maybe they can't afford a real dog," one human boy laughed.

"Give me that rope, this instant!" the teacher yelled.

"I thought we couldn't yell in here?" I reminded her.

I couldn't understand why the class was laughing so hard. Even Orion and his brothers seemed as confused as I was.

Forgetting about the rope, the teacher looked at me with poison in her eyes. She stomped her way behind her table and pulled out a wooden stick. It wasn't very long, but it looked pretty sturdy. I wasn't sure what she was going to do with it as she stomped her way over to me.

"Put out your hands," she demanded.

"My hands?" I asked, confused.

"Yes, your hands," she said, grabbing one of them. "Put them out."

Did she want to see if I had washed them?

Still confused, I put my hands out in front of me and looked at her. Before I could ask why she wanted to see them, she pressed her lips together, raised the stick, and whacked my hands hard with it.

Cory took one giant leap over the table and snatched the stick right out of her grip. "Don't touch her!" he shouted.

The teacher took two steps back, grabbing at her chest. You could hear a pin drop as she looked at Cory with a look of shock in her eyes. Cory huffed and broke the stick across his knee. Seething with anger, he threw the broken stick at the teacher's feet.

In an instant, Zachary was there. He pulled Cory back and whispered something in his ear. I don't know what he said to him, but Cory sat back down after that. I rubbed my hands as the teacher made her way back to her table. The stinging that the stick left behind was now pulsing through my fingers.

"Are you okay?" Delia asked.

I nodded. I couldn't believe the teacher had struck me. Why did she do that? What had I done wrong? Better yet, would she tell my father and get me in trouble. I thought of his words… *"Your punishment will be severe. This will be your only warning."*

I knew I had to tell Cory not to say a word. My father would no doubt ask why the teacher had struck me.

The teacher kept her eyes on Cory as she opened a book that sat upon her table. "Open your books to page thirty-nine," she instructed.

I looked at Cory and Delia. I had no idea what book she was talking about. Too scared to ask, I looked at the humans to see what book they had taken out. I noticed Orion and his brothers were also looking at the humans.

Miri lifted her book and showed it to me. I quickly looked through my bag of books but couldn't find the one Miri was holding up. A loud thump on the table made us all jump back. The teacher was standing over us. She had thrown a book on our table. "You can share that one," she said, still giving Cory an evil eye.

It was like she wanted to rip him apart. Why was she being so mean?

"Begin reading," she said, taking a seat again.

Cory picked up the book and scanned the pages. He put the book in the middle of the table when he found the page the teacher had said to turn to. "Can you guys see it?" Cory asked Orion.

Orion nodded.

"Start reading," Cory instructed.

Still rubbing my hand, I began to read. For the next hour or so, the teacher just sat there, watching everyone read. Anytime I heard her move, I would quickly look up to see if she was about to teach us something. All I found were her eyes on Cory. She wouldn't look away from him. She only tapped her feather on the table and gave Cory dirty looks.

I was glad when she finally said we could close our books. "You may take your afternoon break," she said to everyone. Then she looked at Cory. "With the exception of you," she said very slowly.

"Why can't he come?" I asked.

"Just go, Thea," Cory said. "I'll be fine."

Orion got up and gathered his brothers. Raiden tried running for the door, but his brother, Odin, pulled back the rope.

The teacher jumped to her feet. "Give me that rope, at once," she yelled.

Orion seemed frustrated when he saw the teacher pull out another stick.

"How many of those do you have?" I asked.

The teacher walked from around her table and quickly untied the rope from Raiden's waist.

"Please don't do that," Orion pleaded.

The minute Raiden was free of the rope, he was out the door. His brother, Odin, tried reaching for him, but Raiden was too fast.

"Now look what you've done!" Orion shouted at the teacher.

They both ran out of the classroom, yelling Raiden's name.

"Go, Thea," Cory said, nudging me. "I'll be out as soon as I can."

Once outside, Delia and I finally breathed in a sigh of relief. "That woman is horrible," Delia said, reaching for my hand. "Did she hurt you?"

Before I could answer, I heard Orion calling for his brother. They still hadn't found him.

The human boys laughed. "Is Thirsty lost?" they teased.

Orion and Odin ignored them. "Raiden!" they kept yelling as they ran across the street and into the forest.

I looked around for Miri. When I saw her playing with her friends, I felt my heart break. Why was she ignoring us?

"I don't like school," I said, putting my head down. "I want to go home."

A loud thump came from inside the classroom. Moments later, Cory walked out. His face was beet red. He looked so angry.

"What happened?" Delia quickly asked.

He looked at her from the corner of his eye. "Nothing. I don't want to talk about it."

"Why do you keep rubbing your backside?" Delia asked him.

"Raiden!" we heard again.

Cory ignored her question and grabbed my hand. "Let's help them find their brother," he said, pulling me away.

Chapter Ten: Winners

As we made our way into the forest, I looked over my shoulder at Miri. She was watching us, a sad look on her face. I didn't understand school, or her. It was nothing like I imagined it would be.

I wanted to cry the moment we were in the safety of the trees. I knew the humans would laugh if they saw me sobbing. Before the flood of tears could make their way out, Miri and her brothers were right behind us.

"Are you going home?" Zachary asked.

"What do you care?" Cory shot back.

"I can explain everything," Zachary said, moving closer. "Her father came to our house last night," he said, pointing to me. "He asked us to ignore you guys. He made us promise."

"What?" Delia gasped. "Why would he do that?"

"I don't know," Zachary answered. "But he was very adamant about it."

I looked at Miri, she had tears in her eyes. She slowly moved closer to me and cracked a smile. "Are we still friends, Little Witch?" she asked, reaching for my hand.

Her voice was shaking. I felt her hand trembling as she held mine. I could tell she really did feel bad. I hadn't lost my friend at all.

"Of course, we are," I assured her.

"Did the teacher hurt you?" she asked, looking down at my hand. "It's turning purple."

I hadn't noticed the stick had left a bruise behind. "I'm fine," I said, pulling my hand away.

"I'm sorry the teacher is giving you guys a hard time," Zachary said. "She gets like that sometimes. No one likes her."

"She's a horrible woman," Delia hissed.

"I know," Zachary agreed. "That's why I told Cory to calm down. She would have figured out you guys were witches."

So that's what he whispered to Cory.

"Did you guys do the reading?" Aidan asked. "She'll be asking questions about it later."

The three of us looked at each other. I was sure they had done as much reading as I had—only one page.

"Raiden!" we heard from a good distance away. I couldn't believe they hadn't found him yet.

"We have to go," Cory said, pulling me away again.

"Don't be late," Miri warned. "She'll be furious."

As we made our way through the trees, I tried to put my father out of my head. Why would he ask them to ignore us? I knew Delia and Cory were thinking the same thing.

"What the…?" Cory said, coming to a sudden stop.

I followed his eyes. There, up in a tree, was Raiden. He was sitting on a branch, with hundreds of leaves floating all round him. I instantly knew he was trying to hide from his brothers.

When he chanted a spell, the leaves began to cover his entire body. He giggled as he heard his brothers calling for him.

"I knew it!" Cory said with a big smile. "They really are winners."

"You mean, magical," Delia corrected him.

"You know what I meant," Cory said, releasing my hand.

Cory moved closer to the tree. "Come down now, Raiden. Your brothers are looking for you."

I heard a gasp behind us. It was Orion and Odin. They had a look of shock on their faces. Orion looked up at his brother, then at us, and swallowed thickly.

"What do we do now?" Odin whispered to his brother.

Orion looked at us nervously. "Get ready to run if they start screaming," he answered.

"Why would we scream?" I asked.

Orion's eyes looked like they were about to explode. "Don't be scared, little girl. We're not going to hurt you."

Now I was confused.

"Why would you hurt me?"

"Please don't scream," he pleaded.

"We're not witches," Odin said, shaking his head. "I swear."

"Oh, yes, we are," Raiden said from up in the tree.

Raiden, shut up!" Orion yelled.

Suddenly, Delia burst out in laughter. She almost fell to the ground as we all looked at her confused. "What's so funny?" Cory asked.

She pointed to Orion and Odin, and laughed some more. "They think we're human," she managed to say.

"What?" Cory said, looking at the boys.

Orion didn't know what to make of Delia. "What do you mean; we *think* your human?" he asked.

"What are you?" Odin asked.

"We're wishers," I answered.

"She means, we're winners," Cory explained.

"What?" Orion asked confused.

"We're like you," Delia said, rolling her eyes. "You know, magical."

"Are you trying to say, *witches*?" Orion asked.

I thought it would be easier if I just showed them. I waved my hand and made the leaves that covered Raiden come falling to the ground. I waved it again, sending Raiden floating to his brothers. "I'm flying!" Raiden said, spreading his arms.

"Oh yeah," Cory said, pointing with his thumb. "She's half wizard."

"Hey," I cheered. "We can say, wizard."

Chapter Eleven: The Rope

Cory began to explain why we couldn't say the word, *witch*. When Cory was done, Orion threw his head back and laughed. "I knew there was something off about you guys," he said, shaking his head.

"Tell them about the potion," Odin said to his brother.

"Is that what was in those wooden cups?" Delia asked.

Orion nodded. "Our father made a potion to stop us from telling people we were witches. Raiden's big mouth gets us into a lot of trouble. We've had to move a few times because of him."

Cory was quick to look at me. "Yeah, well this one," he said, pointing with his thumb, "has the same problem, but her father can erase human memories."

I hadn't realized that thumb was meant for me.

"So, her father is really a wizard?" Orion asked.

"Yes, and my mother is a winner," I announced.

"My mother is a witch, too," Raiden informed us. "And, so is my father."

"Looks like the potion wore off," Odin said. We all laughed.

"I'm sorry you got in trouble because of us," Orion said to me. "I didn't know she was going to hit you like that."

"She's horrible," Delia spat.

"I don't want to go back," Raiden said, pulling on his brother's shirt. "I want to go home."

"We can't, Raiden," Orion answered. "We promised father we would try."

"I think we're in the same boat," Cory said.

"We made the same promise," I added. "My father said my punishment would be *severe*."

"Will he hit you?" Raiden asked, concerned.

I made a face. "My father would never hit me. He's never put a hand on me."

Delia rolled her eyes again. "To her, *severe,* is not being able to go outside to play."

"Wow, that is severe," Raiden said, shaking his head.

"Were any of you even able to read?" Delia asked. "She's going to ask questions about it when we get back."

From the looks of it, none of us had read past the first page. "What are we going to do?" Orion asked.

"I have an idea," I said, remembering what my father had done to those books. "I think I know how to fix this, but we'll have to be back in the classroom so I can do it."

"What about the rope?" Odin asked. "Raiden will run away on us again."

Immediately, another idea came to me.

"Hold out your hand," I said to Odin.

"Why?" he asked.

I smiled. "So I can give you a rope."

He reluctantly held up his hand. When I waved my hand, Odin's eyes came alive.

"Hey!" he yelled. "I can feel a rope. I don't see it, but I can feel it."

"Try to run away," I said to Raiden.

It didn't take much convincing. He was off in a flash. He was only able to run a few feet before he was stopped dead in his tracks by his brother, and my invisible rope.

"It worked!" Odin cheered. "You really are a wizard."

Suddenly, a huge smile broke across Cory's face. He snapped his fingers and said… "I have an idea."

He looked at Orion. "Did your father tell you *not* to use magic?"

"Yes, all morning long, why?"

"Because we already broke the rules," Cory answered. "Thea just used her magic. So if we're going to get in trouble, we might as well teach that awful woman some manners."

"I'm in," Orion said with a big smile.

"Are you crazy?" Delia said. "Thea's father will punish her forever."

"No one is going to know that Thea is using magic," Cory explained. "We'll only use it on the teacher, and only harmless spells. The humans will never figure out what's going on."

"No," Delia said, walking away. "I want no part of this."

She began heading back to the school. Cory was right on her heels. "I'll tell William I made her do it. I'll take the blame, I swear it."

"Come on, Thea," Delia yelled. "We're going back to class."

"I bet you'd want to do it if she had hit you," Cory spat.

Delia ignored him and marched her way out of the woods. I had to run to keep up with her. Cory and the boys followed behind us. They seemed very disappointed that Delia hadn't agreed to Cory's plan.

I had to admit, I was also surprised that Cory wanted me to use my magic. He was usually the one who didn't want me to get in trouble. Why was he so willing now?

The humans were still outside playing when we returned. Miss Beady Eyes was already standing on the porch, metal rod in hand. She began hitting the bell.

"We were almost late," Delia said under her breath.

The humans began running into the school. One human boy purposely ripped away one of the patches on Delia's dress as he passed her. He laughed as he threw it over his head and ran inside.

"You idiot!" Delia yelled.

She marched her way up the porch, but Miss Beady Eyes got in front of her. "We do not say such words here, young lady."

~ 80 ~

"But, he tore my dress," Delia explained.

"I saw no such thing," the teacher shot back.

I grabbed the patch that had landed right in front of me. "How about now?" I said, holding it up. "Can you see it now?"

The teacher's beady eyes hardly looked at what I was holding up. "I don't like liars," she said, glaring down at Delia. "Perhaps I should use my ruler on you as well."

Miss Beady Eyes turned on her heels and headed into the classroom. Delia was speechless. She slowly turned to face Cory. "I had better see a nasty wart spell," she grumbled before marching into the class.

Cory almost jumped for joy. He knew Delia had just agreed to his plan. I noticed no one was asking me if *I* agreed to the plan. I didn't want to get in trouble. I knew I had already used my magic, but I had only done it to help out our new friends.

"Thea, follow my lead," Cory instructed, walking into the classroom.

Chapter Twelve: Share

Nervously, I took a seat. What was Cory going to ask of me? Did he want me to turn her into a toad or something? I wasn't sure if I wanted any part of this—even if she had hit me with her stick.

I was still giving Cory's plan some thought when Delia elbowed me. "Thea, she's going to ask questions about the book, remember? What's your plan?"

I had forgotten all about that. I quickly reached for the book the teacher had given us so *nicely*, and closed my eyes. I thought of the words my father had said. I pictured him holding his hands over the books.

"Absorb," I whispered.

Suddenly, my head began to tingle. Soon after, words began flowing through my head. A story was now coming together. Every letter, every phrase, was now entering my waiting brain. I knew the book from beginning to end. It had worked. I had actually pulled it off. This only made me wonder; what else could I do like my father? There had been no streams of light when I did it, but that must have been because my father's magic was much stronger than mine.

"Thea," Delia said, elbowing me again.

I made sure Miss Beady Eyes wasn't looking before I stretched my hand out on the table. "I need you all to touch my hand," I instructed in my lowest voice possible.

I wasn't sure if this was going to work. I had never tried anything like this before.

I thought of all the information I had just absorbed. I looked down at their hands, closed my eyes, and wished all the information into their heads.

"Share," I whispered.

I heard Delia gasp first. Cory just smiled and said, "Wow." Orion gasped even louder than Delia. Odin pulled his hand back and said, "I want to be a wizard." Raiden on the other hand, made a sour face and said, "That's not a happy story."

I made sure the teacher hadn't heard us. She was busy pulling out another one of her sticks. Who was she going to hit now?

I kept my eyes on her as she stood in front of the class. I looked down at her shoes; they were pointy and very ugly. If I didn't know any better, I would say she looked just like a wicked witch.

The class fell silent when she cleared her throat. She slowly began tapping the stick on her palm. With a hint of a smile on her face, she eyed the class. I really think she enjoyed hitting kids with that stick.

"It is quiz time," her voice rang out.

I could hear the class sigh and moan when she said that. I slowly looked at Delia. "What is quiz time?" I asked in a very low voice.

"How should I know," she answered.

"What kind of time is that?" Raiden yelled at the teacher.

The classroom erupted into laughter.

"Silence!" the teacher shouted.

"How come you get to yell?" Raiden asked.

The teacher gave him a death stare. She slowly made her way to our table, the stick held firmly in her hand. "I think I'll start my questions with the six of you," she said, tapping the stick in her palm. "I have a feeling none of you did the reading."

"Sure, we did," Raiden assured her. "I like the part about the witches. They could predict the future. They told the Scottish general he was going to be king one day, but he didn't want to wait. His wife helped him kill the current king, his cousin, when he was sleeping. The general was haunted by that when he became king. In the end, he dies and Malcolm is crowned king of Scotland."

The teacher stood, almost frozen, not knowing what to say. We all looked at each other and smiled. Raiden had done a good job of summing it all up.

I was shocked when the teacher muttered the word, "Impossible."

"He's not lying," Cory shot at her. "That's exactly what happened in the book."

She slowly looked at him. "That book is two hundred and seventy-two pages long, young man. We were on page thirty-nine. No one can read Macbeth that quickly. This class has been reading that book for three weeks."

"Maybe they're slow readers?" I suggested.

Again, the room was filled with laughter.

The teacher looked at us as if we were something to be destroyed. The venom in her beady eyes scared me a little.

"You know what I dislike?" she said, making her way back to her table. "I dislike cheaters. I have no room in my class for children who cheat."

She placed her stick on the table and pulled out an even bigger stick. This one was flat and had a handle on it. What was she going to do with it?

"It's time, Thea," Cory quickly whispered to me. "Give her some hairy warts or something."

I looked back at the teacher, confused by the stick she was holding. When she called Raiden to the middle of the class, I instantly knew she was about to hit him with it.

Anger grew inside of me. Why was she such a horrible person? What had we done to her?

"You're not touching my brother with that thing," Orion growled.

The teacher's eyes almost tore him apart with her glare. "I can, and will, young man. This is my classroom, and I do not tolerate cheaters."

"I'll take his punishment," Cory announced, pushing his chair back. "I'm the one who told him what the book was about."

Shocked, I looked at Cory as he got to his feet. Why was he lying? We hadn't really cheated—much. I was the one who had used magic to read that boring book, not them.

As Cory made his way to the front of the classroom, I began to panic. I couldn't let her hit him. It was time to teach her some manners.

Chapter Thirteen: Manners

A smile spread across the teacher's face as Cory made his way to her. I could see her yellow teeth as he got closer. She was really enjoying this.

"Grab your ankles," she said in her raspy voice.

Cory sighed. He stood frozen for several moments. When he leaned down to grab his ankles, he looked at me from the corner of his eye. I knew that was the signal.

At the moment she raised the stick to hit him, I discreetly waved my hand, sending shock waves into the stick, and up the teacher's arm. Cory almost had to catch her when she dropped the stick and stumbled back.

I looked around to make sure the humans hadn't noticed I was using magic. When I saw them giggling, I knew the coast was clear.

I looked back at the teacher, she was rubbing her arm. "I think my arthritis is acting up," she said mostly to herself.

I was surprised when she reached for the stick again. I looked around, making sure no one was looking my way. "Do it," Delia whispered.

This time, I only waved my finger. I made the stick become hot as coals. When the teacher touched it, you could actually hear a hiss sound at the moment her fingers touched the stick.

She jumped back, flaring her hand around. Cory was trying not to laugh. He gave me an approving nod as he picked up the stick, and tried to hand it to the teacher. "It didn't burn you?" she asked, looking at it.

Cory shrugged his shoulders. "No, it's not hot at all."

I didn't miss the subtle nod Cory gave me as he held out the stick. The teacher nervously reached for it. First, she touched it and quickly jerked her hand back. She tapped it a few more times before taking it from him. The moment Cory's hand was safely away from the stick, I waved my finger again.

"Ouch!" the teacher yelled.

She dropped the stick again and backed away, flaring her hand around. "It's scorching hot!" she yelled.

Again, Cory went to reach for it.

"Not you," the teacher said, stopping him.

She looked around the classroom. "You," she said, pointing at a human boy. "Come here and hand me that stick."

I waved my finger before the dark-haired boy could touch it. The teacher seemed shocked when the boy picked it up and held it out to her.

"It's not burning you?" she asked with a twisted face.

Confused, the boy looked at the stick. "Um, no, ma'am."

She called on another human, this time a curly-haired girl. "Give her the stick," she ordered the boy.

Delia giggled as the teacher's face twisted with confusion. The little girl was now holding the stick. "Nothing?" the teacher asked.

"N…no, ma'am," the little girl answered.

I could hear Zachary and Miri laughing in the back of the classroom. They must have known what I was doing.

"Silence!" the teacher yelled.

She looked at the stick again, not wanting to take it. "Should I grab my ankles?" Cory asked.

She looked at him with such hatred. I was starting to think this woman just didn't like kids, human or not.

"Go sit down," she hissed at Cory. "I'll deal with you later."

I held in my laughter as she made her way back to her table. Delia almost lost it when the teacher wouldn't stop looking over at the stick.

"Thanks, Thea," Cory said, taking a seat next to me. "I don't think I could have taken another swipe with that thing."

"What do you mean; *another* swipe?" I asked.

I thought of the thump I had heard earlier. I looked at the stick that was now lying in the corner of the classroom. "*Grab your ankles*," I heard in my head. Delia's words came next. "*Why do you keep rubbing your backside?*"

I looked at Cory, understanding his need to get back at the teacher. She had struck him with that stick. That's why she asked him to stay behind. No wonder Cory was more than willing to ask that I use my magic.

This changed everything. It was one thing to hit me, but I wasn't going to let her get away with hitting my friends.

I slowly looked at Beady Eyes. Corey could tell that I now knew what she had done. "Thea, no," Cory said, nudging me. "That was enough. We proved our point."

But it was too late for Cory to stop me. I was angry. She had hurt one of my friends. I couldn't wait around to see who she would hurt next. What if Delia was next, or even the humans. They hadn't done anything to her. She was equally as mean to them, too.

"Don't do it, Thea," Delia whispered.

Chapter Fourteen: Havoc

Delia's words did nothing to calm my anger. All I could hear was the pounding of my heart. I knew my father would fry me for this, but that didn't seem to stop me. The injustice Cory had endured at the hands of the teacher was making it difficult to think straight.

How dare she hit him like that? I heard it, almost felt it. She hit him with everything she had. That thump I heard had been loud. She really hurt him. And with that thought, I waved my hand.

"No!" Cory pleaded, trying to stop me.

Before I realized what I was doing, hundreds of spiders came out of the wood work, right behind the teacher's table. My magic had left my fingers faster than I thought.

"Sp…spiders!" a human girl screamed.

The teacher spun around, almost falling off her chair. Screams soon filled the classroom. I waved my hand again, sending the spiders right to Beady Eyes. "Thea, stop it," Cory said, shaking me.

The teacher screamed as the spiders crawled up her legs. In a panic, she began to swat them off of her. I could only hear Raiden's laughter as the teacher stomped on one spider after another.

The last thing I remember was Raiden's voice. "Make the spiders crawl even higher. Make it so they can now breathe fire."

"Raiden, no!" Orion yelled.

In an instant, the spiders began crawling up the walls. Instead of web, the spiders were now releasing fire into the walls. Raiden's fire spell didn't take long to spread all over the ceiling.

"Everyone out!" the teacher shouted.

The humans were stumbling over themselves. One human boy threw a chair and broke a window. "This way!" he shouted, jumping out.

"What did you do?" Delia yelled at me.

"It wasn't me." I quickly answered. "Well, not all of it," I said, looking up at the ceiling.

The fire was spreading quickly. The spiders had already burned away, leaving behind nothing but havoc.

Cory quickly picked me up and tried running for the door, "This way," he told the others.

When we reached the door, Cory had to jump back when flames consumed our only way out. "The window!" Orion said, grabbing his brothers. "We have to get out of here."

It was pointless now. The fire was all around us. It had spread very quickly. Smoke filled the room and made it hard to see. Delia began screaming.

"I'll get us out!" Cory said, trying to calm her.

There were still human children in the classroom. Most of them were coughing and falling to the floor. Soon, we also began to cough. Cory fell to his knees, with me still in his arms. His coughing was getting real bad.

I fell from his arms as he tried to get back up. "I have to get us out of here," he said, falling to his knees again.

"Cory!" Delia cried.

Cory's head hit the floor. He closed his eyes and went to sleep, at least, that's what it looked like. I looked for Orion and his brothers. They had also gone to sleep, with Orion's arms tightly around his brothers.

"Wave your hand," Delia said, sounding out of breath. "Make it go away."

I tried to do what Delia was instructing me. Somehow, my brain wasn't listening to me. I tried to listen for the teacher's instructions as smoke filled my lungs, but she was long gone. She had left us in here and only saved herself. Somehow, that didn't surprise me.

Delia's voice faded. The room became silent as the night. All you could hear were the flames roaring and spreading all around us.

Suddenly, I saw speckles of light surrounding us. At first, I thought they were embers from the burning wood. It took me a moment to realize it was my father's magic. He was here, he was really here.

The speckles floated all around our bodies, making it possible to breathe again. Slowly, I saw the fire being sucked out of the room. Somehow, my father was pulling it out.

Cory began coughing again. He slowly sat up and tried to take in air. He would cough, then try to breathe again. I could see Orion and his brothers doing the same.

As more speckles of light entered the room, the smoke cleared and gave way to fresh air. Breathing became easy. Cory coughed a few more times before jumping to his feet. I was shocked when I heard the sound of something cracking.

At first, I thought the ceiling was about to fall on him. I soon realized the cracking sound was coming from the walls. They began to repair themselves. The burn marks the fire had left behind, quickly disappeared. In a matter of seconds, the room was restored to how it had been. The glass from the broken window was quickly back in place. There was no ash, no sign that there had been a fire just moments ago.

"Are you okay?" Cory asked, helping me to my feet. Before I could answer him, the door flew open. There, standing with a look of panic, was my father.

"Oops," I said, instantly getting behind Cory.

Chapter Fifteen: Big Pickle

The scared me, wanted to run into my father's arms and cry. But the, *in trouble me*, wanted nothing to do with him. I knew I had really done it this time. There was no explaining my way out of it.

I wrapped my hands around Cory's as my father entered the room. He was huffing and puffing as he made his way to me. I braced myself for what was coming. There was no telling what he was about to do to me. I bit my lip and quickly closed my eyes.

Suddenly, my eyes shot open as my father scooped me off my feet. "Thea," my father said in a shaky voice. "You're going to be the death of me." He pulled me closer and wrapped his arms around me. I was safely in his arms. He squeezed me like never before. I could have sworn I saw a tear coming down his cheek as he kissed my head.

"My child," he whispered.

Suddenly, Orion's father burst through the door. He scanned the room in a panic. When he spotted his sons, he was at their side in an instant.

"Are you hurt?" he asked, wrapping his arms around them.

When Orion assured him they were fine, his father instantly grabbed Raiden by the shoulders.

"What have you done?" he yelled.

My father quickly put me on my feet.

"What have *they* done?" my father asked.

Orion's father nervously got to his feet and faced my father. "Don't be scared," he said, putting his hand up. "We're not going to hurt you."

"Hurt me?" my father asked, confused.

Orion's father added, "No need to panic. We're not witches." Preparing for the worse, he stood nervously waiting for my father's reaction.

My father smiled. "That was you, wasn't it? You were the one helping me put out the fire."

This time, the confused look washed across the face of Orion's father. "The one *helping* you?"

"You have nothing to fear from me," my father said, stepping closer. "You are amongst friends."

"They're witches, too," Raiden announced.

"Yeah, but she's a wizard," Odin said, pointing to me.

My father eyed me, almost giving me the, '*I can't believe you told them*,' look. I bit my lip again and looked away from him.

My father slowly peeled his eyes away from me and looked at Orion's father.

"We'd better take care of the mess outside before we demand explanations, don't you think?"

Orion's father looked down at Raiden.

"Agreed," he said, looking back at my father. "My wife, Leslie, is already out there."

"So is Emma, my wife," my father answered.

In that very instant, my mother came storming in with a blonde woman right behind her. The blonde woman ran straight toward Orion and his brothers, while my mother ran towards me. My mother scooped me off my feet and into her arms.

"Thea, are you hurt?" she cried.

I'd never been so happy to see my mother. I knew my father would go a bit easier on me if she was here. Although, I had a feeling nothing was going to get me out of this big pickle.

"Raiden, what did you do?" I heard his mother ask.

My father eyed him before looking back at me. "I suspect the two of you have a lot in common."

I buried my face in my mother's arms. Maybe if I didn't look at him he would just forget this little mishap. A little witch can dream, can't she?

"What happened?" my mother asked.

I bit my lip. It was the one question I was hoping no one would ask. Why couldn't we just forget about this little mess?

"Emma, we must first deal with the humans," my father reminded her.

"Yes, of course," she said, setting me on my feet.

"Wait here," my mother said, following my father out the door.

"We'll be right back," Orion's mother said, following them out.

Their father was last to leave. He gave Raiden one last head shake before walking out.

I was doomed. The minute my father finds out what I had done, he will punish me forever. I will never see daylight or my friends. Never again will I play in the snow with them. Even worse, will he move us away like he had threatened?

I thought about crying, but Raiden beat me to it. "Please don't tell father what I did," he pleaded, pulling on Orion's shirt. "He'll never let me go outside again."

Wow, he was taking the words right out of my mouth. I was about to tell Cory that.

Chapter Sixteen: I like you

I tried to feel bad about what I had done, but truth was, I didn't feel bad at all. I did, however, feel bad about the fire. I never wanted anyone to get hurt. Beady Eyes, on the other hand, had it coming. How could I sit and let her get away with what she had done to Cory.

I looked at Raiden and smiled. Although I hadn't cast the fire spell, I knew his heart was in the right place. He was only trying to help me. He knew how mean that teacher was.

I had made up my mind not to turn him in. I would happily take whatever punishment my father gave me. It had all started with me, and it would end with me. Raiden's parents would never know about his little fire spell.

"You really did it this time, Thea," Delia said. "I think you went too far."

"Why did you start a fire?" Cory asked.

Shocked, I looked at the two of them. How could they think I would burn the place down? Hadn't they heard Raiden casting the fire spell?

"You almost killed us," Cory hissed at me.

"You almost killed everyone," Delia added.

They were angry with me, thinking I had caused the fire. I wasn't expecting that.

"I don't think it was her," Orion said, trying to clear my name. "I heard Raiden casting that spell. I know he didn't mean for it to get this far."

"I only wanted to help," Raiden explained.

"It doesn't matter," Cory answered. "We're all getting in trouble. It was my fault anyway. I'm the one who asked Thea to use her magic."

"No," Delia said, shaking her head. "I'm the one who agreed to it. It's my fault."

Oh, now it *wasn't* my fault? That changed fast.

As we decided whose fault it was, I couldn't help but wonder what my father was doing to fix my mess this time. I knew he would be very disappointed in me. Here I was again, causing him stress and worry. How did I ever get myself into these messes?

"We'll have to move again," Odin said, shaking his head. "I'm so tired of moving."

"I'm sorry, brother," Raiden said, breaking into another sob. "I'm sorry I always get us into trouble. I don't mean to, I swear."

Delia slowly leaned closer to me. "Thea, he sounds just like you."

Her words struck a chord with me. He really did sound like me. I could see he had gotten into as many pickles as I had. That's when I knew I had made the right choice. I wasn't going to let them move again. I planned on taking the whole blame.

I stepped away from Cory and Delia, and made my way to Raiden. I had to tell him to stay quiet. This was going to be our little secret. I was about to lie for him.

"Don't cry," I said, touching his face. "You won't have to move. You see, by the time you had cast your spell, I had already waved my hand. I started that fire, not you."

"You did?" he asked with tears in his eyes.

I winked at him. "Yes, don't you remember?"

Raiden looked deep into my eyes. I was hoping he understood what I was trying to say. There was no point in both of us getting fried.

"But, I heard him," Orion said, cutting in.

"You heard wrong," I said, never looking away from Raiden.

Raiden smiled. "I like you, Thea."

I knew he understood. "And, I like you, too," I answered. "We're going to be very good friends—if I ever get to see you again, that is."

"Yeah, when you're old and grey," Delia said, rolling her eyes.

I swallowed nervously when I heard someone open the door behind me. It was time to face the music. I had to be strong and take the blame, even if it meant never going outside again.

My mother was first to re-enter the room. She looked very worried and tired. She held the door as one by one, human children began floating into the room. They had their eyes closed, put to sleep by my father, no doubt. He was obviously the one making them float.

Miri, Zachary, and Aidan walked in and began telling my mother where everyone had been sitting. "He was over there," Zachary said, pointing to a chair.

My mother guided the floating boy and gently sat him in his chair. Cory stepped away from us and began to help. He grabbed a little girl's foot and pulled her toward him.

"Where was she sitting?" he asked Miri.

"There, next to me," Miri instructed.

Soon, Orion's mother, Leslie, was also helping. I held Raiden's hand until the last of the humans were safely in their seats. They all looked like they were just taking a nap.

"We can't leave anything behind," Leslie said, looking around the classroom. "Where are your cups?" she asked her boys.

"Behind that table," Orion said, pointing.

"Thea, grab your book bag," my mother ordered. She sounded upset.

"Yes, Mother."

"Are we leaving?" Delia asked.

"Yes," my mother answered. "You were never here—none of you were," she said, looking at us all.

"There's no time to spare," Leslie said to my mother while gathering up her boys. "Our husbands can't keep that shield up forever."

Before I could move, the teacher came floating in. Her hair was a tangled mess. Her shoes were half on and hanging off her toes. My mother quickly used a spell to fix the woman's hair. She slipped her shoes back on before sitting the teacher at her table.

As she carefully straightened out the woman's collar, my mother said, "Everyone out."

I threw my heavy book bag over my shoulder, looking back at the classroom. I really wanted this to work out. I never intended for things to get this bad. I wanted to make my father proud; show him I could be the little witch he always wanted me to be.

"Off we go, Thea," my mother said, reaching for my hand.

Miri waved goodbye as she took her seat.

"I'll see you later, Little Witch."

Chapter Seventeen: It's Time

The moment we walked outside, I could see what my father was doing. He still had his eyes closed, his arms still in the air. He was keeping a shield on the school so the town couldn't see the fire. He made sure no one would know what had happened.

Orion's father was also using magic, but his magic was nothing like my father's. Orion's father had to cast spells for his magic to work. My father was the most powerful wizard around here, with magical abilities others could only dream of.

Orion's father stopped casting spells when he saw us walking out of the school house. My father didn't open his eyes until we were safely in the trees.

"We're out, William," my mother yelled.

When my father opened his eyes, the ground shook once. He quickly made his way to us and ordered each of us to stay behind a tree.

"I must make sure all is well," he said, looking toward the school.

My mother held her breath as my father waved his hand in the direction of the school. I wasn't sure what he was waiting for. Then I saw them, the humans calmly walking out of the classroom. They began leaving the grounds like nothing had happened.

"It's three o'clock," Cory whispered. "I think they're going home."

Delia drew breath when the human boy who had torn her patch walked right by us. He didn't give us a second glance. It was like he didn't recognize us at all.

I looked at my father, knowing he had erased us from their memories.

Leslie, Orion's mother, began to cry.

"It's over," she said, throwing herself into her husband's arms.

"Don't cry," the father said, holding her tight. He kept looking at my father. He seemed amazed at what he witnessed my father do. "You really are a wizard, aren't you?"

My father smiled. "And you are really a witch."

"My name is Tobias," the father said, offering his hand. "I am indebted to you."

My father shook his hand. "I am William, and you owe me nothing."

Tobias looked down at Raiden. "I'm afraid my son is to blame for this," he said, looking back at my father.

"You haven't met my daughter, have you?" my father answered. "I have a feeling you will change your mind when I explain things to you."

"That's funny," Tobias said, shaking his head. "I was about to say the same thing to you."

They shared a laugh.

"But first," my father said, glaring down at me. "I'm getting to the bottom of this."

I bowed my head. Although I felt bad about it, it was time to lie to my father.

"I started the fire," I confessed.

"Thea," my mother gasped.

I swallowed thickly when my father leaned down, grabbed my shoulders tightly, and ordered me to look at him.

I had tears in my eyes when I saw the disappointed look on his face. He was so angry with me. I'd never seen him look at me like that before.

"Thea," he said through his teeth. "What possible reason could you have for almost burning those innocent children today?"

"I didn't mean for the fire to spread like that, I swear."

He tightened his grip on me. "You could have killed your friends today— killed them," he said, pointing to Orion and his brothers. "Why did you do it?" he shouted.

"William," my mother said.

My father was furious. He ignored my mother as he squeezed my arms tighter. "I asked you a question," he yelled.

"Answer him, Thea," my mother pleaded.

I slowly looked into my father's eyes. They were burning a hole right through me.

"Because the teacher was being mean to us," I finally answered.

My father was silent for a few moments. He didn't seem pleased with my answer. He slowly let me go and rose to his feet. "I am going to do something I may regret, Thea. But I think it's time, time I took a belt to you."

"William, no," my mother gasped.

"You can't," Cory said, stepping in front of me. "I can explain everything."

"Not this time, Cory," my father said, pushing him aside.

My father grabbed my arm and began almost dragging me home. He was walking so fast, I was having a hard time keeping up with him.

"Please, let me explain," Cory kept saying.

Raiden began crying as we walked away.

"It was me," he confessed. "Please don't hit her. I'm the one who did it."

It was too late. My father didn't believe him. It was obvious he thought Raiden was only trying to get me out of this pickle.

"Please," Cory said following behind us. "Just let me show you something."

"Go home, Cory," my father shouted.

We left the others behind as my mother still pleaded with my father. He wasn't having it. He ignored everything she said to him.

I couldn't believe he was about to punish me like that. Never in a million years did I think he would ever lay a hand on me. My luck had finally run out. Being kept inside didn't seem so bad now.

"Please, let me explain," Cory begged, all the way back to our cottage.

Chapter Eighteen: Never be Afraid

My mother tried to pull me away from my father the minute we walked into the cottage. Cory was still pleading with him.

"Just let me show you something," he kept saying.

"You're not seriously going to hit her, are you?" my mother asked.

"I have to!" my father yelled. "Don't you realize what she almost did? You can't save her from this one, Emma."

"William, she's just a child."

He glared at her. "A child that almost killed a room full of children. And why? Just because the teacher was not to her liking?"

"It wasn't like that," Cory tried to explain. "I was the one who asked her to use her magic. She didn't want to do it."

"What are you saying?" my father asked.

Cory sighed. "If you would just let me show you something. It would explain everything."

"You have two minutes," my father said, finally agreeing to listen to him.

Cory took a deep breath and began to unbuckle his belt. "Thea, turn around," he said holding up his pants.

I spun around, but looked over my shoulder when I heard my mother gasp. I couldn't believe it. Cory's backside was black and blue. The teacher had hit him harder than I thought.

"What in the world?" my mother said, as Cory pulled his pants back up.

"The teacher hit Thea, too," Delia said from the door. "Look at her hands."

"What?" my mother gasped.

My father's face became red with fury. He stood paralyzed for several long moments. His hand was shaking as he reached for mine. "Show me your hands, Thea," he said softly.

I didn't want to show him. I knew it would only get me in more trouble. I put my hands behind my back and shook my head no.

My father leaned down. His voice became softer, friendlier. "Why don't you want to show me?"

I looked at the floor. "Because you said my punishment would be severe this time."

I looked up, my father had his eyes closed. My mother, on the other hand, was giving him the death stare.

"Please, show me your hands," he asked again. "I give you my word, you will not be punished."

"Show us, Thea," my mother pleaded.

I slowly held out my hands. My father was shaking as he turned them over and saw the bruises. "Oh my goodness," my mother said, putting her hand over her mouth.

"The teacher hit her with a stick," Delia informed them. "And, she hit her hard."

My father held up his hand. "Please, Delia. That is not helping me stay calm."

He looked down at my hands again, holding his gaze there for several long moments. "Why did she hit you?" he asked in a shaky voice.

"I'm not sure," I answered. "The class was laughing, and she, well, asked me to hold out my hands."

My mother quickly headed for the door. "Emma, no!" my father yelled. "She won't remember who you are."

My mother stopped dead in her tracks. She was fuming. "How dare she touch my child," she hissed.

My father sighed. He ran his fingers through his hair. "I don't understand, Thea. Why didn't you leave and come running home? Why didn't you come tell us?"

"I thought you would be angry with me," I explained.

My words seemed to crush my father. There was a look of pain all over his face. I was surprised when he gathered me in his arms.

"Forgive me, Thea. Forgive me for making you feel like you couldn't tell me." He pulled away. "I was wrong for casting fear in your heart. I don't ever want you to think you can't come to me for help; especially if someone puts their hands on you. Never be afraid to tell me."

He pulled me into his arms again. "I will always be on your side, Thea. I am your father, and I will always defend you. I want you to understand how wrong that teacher was for hitting you. She had no right to do that. You understand that, don't you?" he asked, pulling away again.

"You're not angry with me?" I asked.

"I am, but for other reasons. You should have never started that fire. You put many lives in danger."

I put my head down again. I felt my father's fingers on my chin. "Look at me, Thea," he said, lifting my chin. "It really wasn't you, was it?"

There was no point in lying.

"I only made spiders come out of the walls," I admitted. "Raiden is the one who made them breathe fire."

My father smiled. "Somehow, I'm not surprised."

"She only did it because the teacher was about to hit Cory again," Delia explained. "We were trying to teach her some manners."

"I made Thea do it," Cory fessed up. "But, only because she had already hit me."

"And, she was mad because we read the book to the end," Delia continued. "Thea absorbed it and shared it with us."

My heart almost leaped out of my chest. I wanted to tell Delia to shut up.

"Absorbed it?" my father asked.

I was done for. How was I going to explain that?

"Thea?" my father said. "Where did you learn how to do that?"

Cory spoke up before I could say a word. "We saw you in the forest," he explained. "You had all those books, and we saw you doing it."

"Hmm," my mother said giving him another death stare.

My father raised an eyebrow to her. "I know, Emma. I know."

My father rose to his feet when someone knocked on our door.

"Come in," my father called.

As soon as the door was opened, Raiden came storming in. "Don't hit her! It was me. It was me," he said, heading straight to my father.

Before Raiden could reach him, he was pulled back and fell to the ground.

"Odin, let go of the invisible rope," Raiden yelled to his brother.

"Invisible rope?" my father asked confused.

"Oops," I said, closing my eyes.

Chapter Nineteen: Treehouse

Tobias, Orion's father, had invited us to their house for supper. Everyone seemed to be in a good mood now. I was up in the treehouse with Delia and the boys. My father and Tobias were sitting just beneath us, talking on a bench. My mother was inside the house with Leslie, helping her make dinner.

I could hear my father's laughter as Tobias told him of all the troubles Raiden had gotten himself into. It was like a competition between them. My father would say, "I have a better one for you. Thea actually kidnapped a man she believed to be Santa Claus."

Their laughter echoed throughout the massive yard. They told one story after the other.

"I hope my father tells him the one about the hunters," Raiden said.

Of course, we were listening. I liked hearing the stories about Raiden. He was my kind of kid.

"What's so special about the hunters?" I asked.

Odin rolled his eyes. "Every time they took aim at a deer, Raiden here would cast a spell and make the deer say...bang."

I laughed real hard at that one. I couldn't get over how much like me, Raiden really was.

"Hey, look, your human friends are coming over." Orion said, pointing toward Miri and her brothers.

My father was still laughing when Miri got there. "Do we still have to ignore them?" she asked.

My father smiled. "No, and thank you for listening to me."

"Why did you want us to ignore them in the first place?" Zachary asked. "I think we hurt their feelings."

"I apologize for that, young man. You see, I didn't want to put you at risk. I knew if Thea somehow found a way to tell people she was a witch, they would also accuse you, if they knew you were friends."

"I understand now," Zachary answered.

"So, can we play with them now?" Miri asked.

"There's plenty of room up here," Raiden yelled.

I instantly felt happier. I had my friends back. As it turns out, my father was only trying to protect them.

We spent the day playing in the treehouse. Orion was shocked when Zachary asked if I had taken them flying yet.

"You can fly?" Raiden asked, amazed.

"Oh no," Delia said, rolling her eyes. "Please don't show him how to fly. We'll never find him."

We all erupted into laughter.

"Dinner," my mother called.

We came down from the treehouse in a flash. I was overjoyed when Leslie invited Miri and her brothers to stay for supper.

We had supper outside, under the stars. Although the ground was covered in snow, it somehow felt warm and inviting outside. My father and Tobias had started a fire. My mother had already placed a pot of tea over the flames.

We took our places on a long wooden table. I hadn't realized just how hungry I was.

Leslie was an excellent cook. She made a stew which she served in a bowl made of bread. My mother prepared her famous biscuits, so it didn't surprise me when my father was the first to reach for one.

"Excellent, as always, Emma," he said lovingly.

It was the perfect night. Perfect until Tobias asked about school. "We're not sending them back there again, are we?" he asked my father.

My father gave it some thought. "I still believe we need to teach our children more about the human world. Today was a perfect example of how little they are prepared."

"We can't send them back to that woman," my mother quickly hissed at him.

"Of course not," my father agreed. "I think we should do it slowly. Perhaps prepare them better this time. I think if they had a better teacher, they would do well."

My mother snorted. "I knew that woman was no good. She wasn't very nice to us, either."

"I think we all feel the same," Leslie said, placing some spoons on the table. "It sounds like that woman has no business teaching children."

"She's horrible," Miri said with a mouth full of stew. "She whacks at least one kid every week."

"And those rulers," Aidan said, shaking his head. "She loves using them."

"Is that what she calls her stick?" Cory asked. I heard her saying that word."

"That's not its name, it's a ruler," Aidan explained. "You know, to measure things?"

"Like what?" I asked taking a mouth full of stew.

He shrugged his shoulders. "I don't know, things that need to be measured, I guess."

"Why, can't you tell how long something is?" Raiden asked.

"My point exactly," my father said, shaking his head.

"Feel bad for *us*," Zachary said, pointing to himself. "We still have to go back there."

I noticed the look my mother exchanged with my father. "I assure you," my father said. "You won't have to worry about her temper again."

"What are you going to do, show *her* the stick?" Aidan asked.

My father laughed. "Vengeance is not healthy for the soul, young man."

"So, what *are* you going to do to her?" Cory asked.

Again, my father exchanged glances with my mother.

"Why don't we just enjoy this night," Tobias said, reaching for his stew.

We soon forgot all about school and talked into the night. I was glad Raiden hadn't gotten in trouble for casting that fire spell. His father was quick to explain why that spell was bad. Raiden agreed to never use it again.

After the last biscuit was gone, my mother helped Leslie clear the table. Tobias kept looking at my father. "May I ask you something," he said.

"Certainly," my father answered.

"How did you erase their memories? How is it possible they will never remember us? A spell like that would save us from having to move so much," he said, glancing at Raiden.

My father chuckled. "Yes, I understand. But, it wasn't a spell, at least, not a spell you can cast. But I will, however, teach you one that will be of good use to you." My father looked at Raiden and shook his head. "I'm sure you'll find yourself using it from time to time."

They both laughed.

Tobias reached across the table and offered my father his hand. "Thank you, friend."

My father shook his hand, "Friend."

After some more talk, my father thanked Leslie for the fine meal and we said goodnight. My mother made them promise they would come to our house for supper next. Raiden was very happy about that.

After walking Zachary, Miri, and Aidan home, we headed to Delia's house.

"He's probably not even home," I heard my mother say under her breath.

I knew she was talking about Delia's father. It was very rare for him to be home. Most of the time, poor Delia was left alone. I was sure this night wouldn't be any different from any other.

As we walked through the woods to Delia's house, we heard a grumbling sound coming from a few feet away. My mother quickly gathered us close to her as my father left to investigate what it was.

I kept my eyes on him as he walked toward the sound. Suddenly, he stopped dead in his tracks.

"What is it?" my mother asked.

My father looked half way over his shoulder. "Take them home, Emma. I'll be along shortly."

"Is everything okay?" my mother asked.

"That's my father's coat," Delia said, pointing to a nearby bush.

Delia broke free of my mother's hand and ran toward my father. My father quickly turned and tried to stop her. It was too late. My father bowed his head as Delia looked down at her father. Her eyes quickly filled with tears. "What's wrong with him?" she asked.

"Oh, no," I heard my mother say.

I could smell the alcohol from here. He was drunk and passed out in the snow.

"I'll go help," Cory said, joining them.

Delia kept her head down, tears streaming down her face. My mother clutched at her heart and gently pulled Delia away.

"Come, Delia. Let's go home."

I looked over my shoulder to see Cory helping my father lift Delia's father up from the snow. Delia never looked back.

Chapter Twenty: Nice

It was a quiet walk back to our cottage. I didn't know what to say to Delia. I knew she was in pain right now. How I wished there was something I could do. My mother's eyes filled with tears every time she looked down at poor Delia.

When we reached our cottage, my mother asked if we wanted some cookies. I knew she was only trying to cheer Delia up.

"I'll make a fire and we can talk," my mother said, opening the door.

"I want to go to bed," Delia said, with her head down.

She let go of my mother's hand and ran into my room. My mother put her hand over her heart. "Oh, Delia," she cried.

I slowly walked into my room to find Delia standing by my window. She had her back to me, but I could hear her crying.

"Maybe he was just tired?" I said, trying to make an excuse for him.

Delia put her head down. "You think that's the first time I've seen him like that?" She looked out the window again. "Funny how your father always seems to know and brings me here."

"You mind if I stay here tonight?" I heard Cory say.

"Yes, just give me a moment." It was my father. They were back.

"May I come in?" he asked from the doorway.

"Yes, Father."

He walked across the room and sat at the edge of my bed. "Delia," he said softly. "Will you come sit next to me, please?"

Delia slowly turned and sat next to him. My father put his arm around her and kissed her head.

"I don't want you to be sad," he began. "Your father isn't a bad man. He's just in pain."

Delia looked into his eyes. "What do you mean?"

He sighed. "I knew your father when he didn't drink. He was a good man back then, but when he lost your mother, I witnessed him falling apart. I strongly believe that drinking is his way of easing the pain in his heart. He's just lost, Delia, but I know he truly loves you."

"I lost her, too," Delia cried. "He's not the only one who's in pain."

My father gathered her in his arms. "I wish I could bring her back," he whispered. "But what I can do is give you back your father."

"What?" Delia said, wiping her tears.

My father smiled. "It's time I help him find himself; time I help him find, *you*."

Delia looked confused. My father touched her face. "Sometimes we don't realize what we have, until it's gone."

I was surprised when he tapped her on the head. Delia instantly got a faraway look on her face. She looked dazed.

"What did you do to her?" I asked.

My father rose to his feet. "She'll be fine in just a moment," he assured me. "Don't remind her about what she saw tonight, understand?"

"Yes, Father," I said, looking at Delia.

"Cory," my father called. "You may come in now."

I kept my eyes on Delia. She seemed to be coming out of it now. I knew my father had erased what she had seen. I just wasn't sure what else he had erased.

"Remember what I said," my father said to Cory.

"Yes, Sir."

"Oh, is Cory staying here tonight?" I heard Delia ask.

She touched her eyes. "Hey, why are my eyes all wet?"

"I believe Thea threw a snowball at you," my father said, walking out.

By morning, I was still wondering what my father was going to do. Delia hadn't said a word about her father all night. We had stayed up talking, laughing at all the stories about Raiden.

"He's like the boy version of you," Delia had said to me.

I was quick to make my bed and dress myself. Cory and Delia were already waiting at the table for breakfast. I could already smell my mother's cooking.

"Morning," I said, taking my place at the table.

"Good morning," my father said with a big smile. "Are the three of you ready to go into town today?"

I instantly became nervous. "We're not going to school, are we?"

He smiled wider. "Actually, we are."

"What?" Cory gasped.

"William," my mother said, giving him a look. "Don't scare them like that."

My mother stroked my hair. "We're only stopping by, Sweetie."

How could I eat after that? I didn't want to go anywhere near that school. I could see Delia and Cory felt the same.

"Why do you suppose we're going there?" Cory asked as we walked through the woods.

"Maybe your father is going to put a horrible curse on her," Delia suggested. "You know, like the one that makes her face look like a toad, and every time she yells at us, she croaks."

I knew she was wrong when my father laughed at what she said.

The ground to play on was full of human children when we arrived. That meant Miss Beady Eyes hadn't hit her bell yet.

"Come along, Thea," my mother said, pulling me toward the school.

I was shocked when we began making our way inside. What was my father going to do?

Miss Beady Eyes was sitting at her table when we walked in. My mother slammed the door behind us and glared at her.

Startled, the teacher snapped her ugly head our way. As usual, she didn't look very happy. "How may I help you?" she hissed.

My mother let go of my hand, pressed her lips together, and slowly made her way to her table. "On your feet, witch," my mother ordered.

"Excuse me?" the teacher said, removing her glasses. "Who do you think you are?"

My mother smiled. "You can stand on your own, or I can make you. Pick one."

"What is the meaning of this?" the teacher asked, getting to her feet. "Leave my classroom, at once."

My mother moved closer. "You had us all fooled, witch. You even fooled my husband for a little while. Too bad he wasn't close enough to you this morning to sense it."

"What are you talking about?" Beady Eyes answered.

"You picked a good hiding place," my mother said, moving even closer. "It was brilliant of you to hide right under their noses. No one would have ever suspected that *you* were a witch."

My jaw dropped. So I had been right about her all along. She really was a wicked witch.

I thought Beady Eyes was going to pass out.

"I…I don't know what you're talking about?" she sputtered, backing away.

"Thing is," my mother continued. "You never thought real witches would bring their children here. You thought you could hide here forever. You're one of those witches that hates humans, especially children. It is witches like you that give witches like me, a bad name."

"You have it all wrong," Beady Eyes answered. "I'm not a witch."

Again, my mother moved closer. "It was almost a perfect plan. Perfect, until you touched my child. Only a witch can leave behind a scent like that. Fortunately, my husband was wise enough to catch that little mistake of yours."

I thought her head was going to explode, when my mother said that. She knew it was over.

Suddenly, she tried running for the door. My father waved his hand and sent her sliding across the floor, and right into the wall. I heard her huff once before the wall was "kind" enough to knock her out.

My father waved his hand again, sending a ray of light directly at her. I wasn't sure what that ray was for, but my father seemed pleased about it.

"Help me with her," my father said to Cory.

I watched as they placed her back in her chair. "Come, Thea," my mother said, grabbing my hand. "It's time to go home now."

"What did he do to her?" Delia asked.

My mother looked at Beady Eyes. "You'll see," she said, leading us away.

I was very confused as we waited near the school. What was supposed to happen? I wanted to ask, but I knew my father wouldn't tell me.

"She's coming out," my mother said, pointing.

I spun around, it was Beady Eyes—only her eyes didn't look beady anymore. In fact, she was even smiling. She began to hit the bell.

"Time for class!" her voice rang out.

Her voice sounded friendly, sweet, even. I watched in shock, as she smiled at every human who walked by her. "Did you all have fun?" she asked.

The humans seemed as shocked as I was. One human boy pulled away from her in fear, when she tried to pat him on the head. "What a good boy," she said, almost cheering.

"Wow," Cory gasped. "I can't believe my eyes. She's actually *nice.*"

"And, *nice,* she will stay," my father answered.

I kept looking back at the teacher as my mother pulled me away. She was a different woman, pleasant, in fact. This only gave me hope for Delia's situation. If my father could change a woman like her with a wave of his hand, imagine what he could do to Delia's father.

I smiled at the thought of that, knowing that Delia would never be alone again.

"Raiden!" we heard a good distance away.

"Here we go again," Delia said, rolling her eyes.

CPSIA information can be obtained
at www.ICGtesting.com
Printed in the USA
BVHW031013280822
645711BV00014B/529

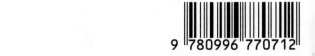